SAVE THE DATE

Save the Date

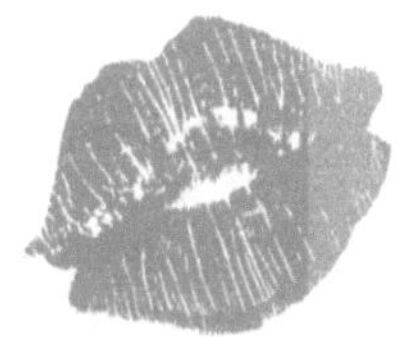

JILLIAN DODD

Editor: Jovana Shirley, Unforeseen Editing, www.unforeseenediting.com

Jillian Dodd Inc.
Seminole, FL

ISBN: 978-1-962549-45-5

BOOKS BY JILLIAN DODD

Eastbrooke Academy®
Best Friends Aren't Forever
Popularity Isn't Easy
Kisses Don't Stay Secret
First Loves Are Hard To Forget

London Prep®
The Exchange
The Boys' Club
The Kiss
The Key
The Party
The Country House
The Choice
The Club
The Match

The Keatyn Chronicles®
Stalk Me
Kiss Me
Date Me
Love Me
Adore Me
Hate Me
Get Me
Fame
Power
Money
Sex
Love
A Very Keatyn Christmas
Keatyn Unscripted
Aiden

That Boy®
That Boy
That Wedding
That Baby
That Love
That Ring
That Summer
That Promise
That Forever
That Crush
That Girl
That Someday

Dating in the City
Writing Mr. Right
Heart Stopper
Crazy For You
Catching Feelings
Party of One
Save the Date
Urban Cowboy
Check, Please!
Happily Ever Afters

Crawford Brothers
Vegas Love
Broken Love
Fake Love

Spy Girl®
The Prince
The Eagle
The Society
The Valiant
The Dauntless
The Phoenix
The Echelon

Girl off the Grid

Chapter One

"SO, I HAVE some news about work," Hayley calmly says while rooting through my closet.

It's been a few months since her inappropriate relationship with her boss came to an end when he was found sleeping with another staff member and got fired, so I can't imagine it could have anything to do with that.

"Spill it."

"Well … I might or might not be in consideration for junior associate depending on the outcome of a case I'm working on," she says distractedly while pulling out another sundress.

"Hayley! Are you serious? That's awesome."

"I know. I'm in shock. I don't want to jinx it, but I had to share." She grabs my arms, and we start jumping up and down, practically trampling the clothes strewn all over my bedroom floor.

"They must have noticed your hard work and all those hours you've been putting in. I told you your brilliance and talent would pay off someday."

"Well, I don't want to celebrate yet. Since my old boss was fired, I've been doing all I can to show the new guy how professional and capable I am. I won't know until after we get back from the wedding how this will play out."

I hold up a long, flowy sundress, my eyebrows raised. "Is this worthy of a fabulous island resort?"

"For sure. You'll look awesome."

"You mean that?" I can't help but feel a tiny bit skeptical. I mean, sure, I'm a best-selling author, and my grandmother has more money than God, but that doesn't mean I'm accustomed to fancy-schmancy destination weddings at resorts that look like something out of a dream.

My eyes just about fell out of my head when Hayley first showed me the website for the resort at which her sister is getting married in a little over a week. Pristine white sand, water so clear that you can see straight through it to the bottom, infinity pools, jaw-dropping views of lush mountainsides in the distance.

And she's taking me as her plus-one because she's the best friend in the entire world, and neither one of us has a man in our lives right now, but I fully expect there will be plenty of men interested the second Hayley sits by the pool.

"You look awesome in just about everything, as if you didn't know," she chides with a grin before sorting through the handful of bathing suits in front of her.

I normally buy a new one every year, though I almost never have a reason to wear one. Weird, I know—though that's hardly the weirdest thing about me.

"Anything worthwhile in the pile?"

"They're all cute as hell. I'd have to see them on you though."

"Eek. I didn't know I'd actually have to wear them."

She laughs. "Kitty."

"I'll probably wear a cover-up most of the time anyway. I have a couple of adorable caftans. I'll look fabulous when sitting by the pool, sipping a fruity cocktail under a dramatic sun hat."

"You're young and gorgeous and hot. Why spend your time lounging in a caftan and sun hat when you can dive into the pool and make a dramatic exit with water pouring off your bronzed skin?"

Nice mental image, but it doesn't stop me from snorting in disbelief. "Honey, I think you have your life and my life mixed up. I love you, I do, but you're the bronzed goddess. I'm the girl walking behind you, slipping and falling on the water dripping from your skin."

She laughs before throwing a balled-up bikini top at me. "Shut up. It's almost boring, how hard you are on yourself. You're beautiful, and you know it. You need a little confidence."

"I need a lot of things."

"Once we get there, you'll see. You're just as hot as any of the other girls who'll be there."

I bite my tongue since arguing isn't getting me anywhere. It's not that I think of myself as an ogre. It's more like I've never seen myself as the type who lounges gracefully by the pool, being waited on hand and foot, catching the eye of a tanned stranger in a lounge chair across the way and beckoning him with a sly smile.

Dang it. Even my *this will never* happen fantasies end up looking like a romance-novel setup. Call it habit.

She stands with a satisfied look on her face. "I think a quick shopping trip is all you'll need, and don't even bother pouting and grumbling."

"Not even a little?"

"Not even a little. You need something to wear to the actual wedding and maybe the rehearsal dinner, but I think you'll be okay otherwise." She goes to the vanity, where my jewelry box is open, and toys with a few pairs of earrings.

"What about activewear? Like sneakers and shorts. Didn't you say there are tours and stuff on the schedule?"

She pulls a face that I catch sight of in the mirror. "Yawn. You can tell my mom had a hand in planning this event. Why we have to be there for a week is a mystery to me. The rest of the guests won't even show up until right before the wedding. Two days at most."

Only she would complain about a week in paradise. I, on the other hand, know a good deal when it lands in my lap. "Come on. It could be fun. Life can't be all lounging by the pool and ordering daiquiris."

"You close your lying mouth," she warns, snapping the box shut. "I refuse to hear such blasphemy."

"Come on." I laugh, stepping over the piles of clothes. "Let's get something to eat. I'm famished from all this planning."

It's easy for me to feel lighthearted right now. My latest book hit the market last week, and my editor is pleased with the sales so far. I'm thankfully back on the calendar for the rest of the year and starting to get used to this quick-turnaround business. I can afford to feel smiley and generous.

We're on our way to dinner, walking in the early March sunshine, when Hayley brings up what's been on my mind. "So, it looks like they're pushing your e-books pretty hard. Your publisher, I mean."

"You noticed that, huh?"

"I've seen a few ads for your latest. I guess I'm part of the target audience." She rolls her eyes and blows out a heavy sigh. "As if I would be caught dead reading romance."

I know she's joking. It's a common misconception that only bored housewives read them, but nothing could be further from the truth.

"E-books save on publishing costs, I guess. And the turnaround is quicker since there's no waiting for print and shipping to stores." Not that my books aren't in stores, but I've noticed the trend too. And not only with my books.

"Let's face it; we live in a *now, now, now* world. Nobody wants to wait to get what they want. They want it immediately downloaded on their e-reader, so they can read on the toilet—the way God intended."

"What a lovely thing to say."

"Hey, if you can help just one reader through a difficult bathroom trip, wouldn't you say it was worth the effort of writing the book?" She flashes a wicked grin while opening the door to a nearby restaurant, where they happen to serve nachos worthy of epic love poems.

"You are so darn charming sometimes. Not exactly what I want on my mind when I'm minutes away from eating."

"Oh, please. I could describe a dismemberment in graphic detail, and you'd listen while dragging your finger through the last of the guacamole—and don't even pretend otherwise."

She's not wrong.

It doesn't take long for me to figure out why Hayley started talking about my work either. "I should've known," I groan when the spinner comes out of her purse. "You don't usually bring up business out of nowhere."

"Well, you know Maggie's going to start asking about the next book, if she hasn't already."

"I was hoping to wait until after the wedding, to

be honest. A nice little vacation to recharge the batteries and all that. And I might end up with inspiration after spending a week in the lap of luxury. Who knows?"

She taps a finger on the spinner, which is now between us on the table. "It'll be easier to put your inspiration to use if you already have a hero in mind, right? And, hey, what if you happen to meet somebody at the resort who falls in line with who you're supposed to be dating next?"

I guess she has a point though really. It would be nice to just meet somebody and date them without the ulterior motive of writing a new book dangling over my head. After almost a year of dating for business—though there's been pleasure; don't get me wrong—I'm getting tired of feeling like my personal life and my career are permanently intertwined.

Still, I know darn well she'll never let it go. I won't leave the restaurant with all my body parts intact if I don't play along. "Okay, fine, you win. Let's see who I'm writing about this time."

"I'll spin it for you." She's already flicked the wheel, spinning through trope after trope without giving me a chance.

"Wow, you're eager. Maybe you should be the one to date whoever the lucky guy happens to be."

"I'm always interested in who you end up with, and you know it. Besides, I'm the one who came up with the idea to use this thing."

We both look down at the spinner once it arrives at the next trope I have to tackle.

And my foot shoots out to kick Hayley's shin under the table.

"Ouch!" she yelps before kicking me back.

"You rigged it!"

"Did not."

"I know you did." I snatch the device from the table before she can grab it and then scroll through the list of tropes written down for me to choose from. Sure enough, every single one of them is the same.

Best Man.

When I look at her, shooting a glare that could melt steel, she shrugs and slumps a little in her chair. "He's amazing. I know the two of you will hit it off."

"You erased all the tropes and added nothing but *Best Man*, so there wouldn't be a choice. That's not fair."

"He's gorgeous and Zack's best friend. Kylie loves him, and trust me, my sister is a hard sell. I've hung around him a few times at parties at their place. He's a really nice guy, Mr. All-American. Works in finance. I wouldn't recommend you date just anybody."

"He might be your future brother-in-law's best friend, and he might be really nice, but that doesn't mean I appreciate you forcing me into dating him."

"Fine. Suit yourself. If my vote of confidence

isn't good enough for you …" She sits back, folding her arms and pouting.

"You know, our server's going to trip over that bottom lip of yours if you stick it out any farther."

She does it anyway, just to spite me. "You're no fun."

"What's his name?"

She wrinkles her nose. "You're gonna hate it."

"Oh, this bodes well."

"Briggs."

I can't help it. A laugh bursts out from between my pursed lips. "So, a prep-school preppy?"

"Who says he went to prep school?"

"Knowing your sister and the sort of people she hangs around …"

Kylie is a financial wizard. Basically Hayley with darker blonde hair and slightly less sparkly eyes and a knack for numbers instead of law.

"Okay, he went to prep school. Happy? That doesn't mean he's not super nice.

"And obviously, his first name isn't Briggs. That's his last name. Everybody just calls him by it."

"I won't."

"Great. I'm sure the two of you are going to hit it off famously if that's the attitude you insist on taking."

"Does he wear polo shirts with the collar popped?"

That earns me an eye roll.

"He's not the villain from an '80s teen comedy,

Kitty."

"I at least have to know his real first name. I can't take him seriously without knowing his actual name. I'm sorry. Those are the rules."

She shakes her head. "I'll see if I can find out, though something tells me my sister has a lot more on her mind than that right now."

"Would finding out this dude's real first name take that much time out of her busy pre-wedding schedule?"

"You don't know my sister. You think I'm Type A?" Hayley snickers, shaking her head though there's obvious affection in her voice. "You have yet to meet the ultimate. Her brain is like a computer that's always running twenty programs at a time. Like having a million tabs open in a browser all at once, while playing some weird music or video in the background. I'd hate to be inside her head."

Meanwhile, I'm sitting here, thinking I'd like to get to know her better.

I'll have plenty of time to do that once we're at the resort, I guess.

Chapter Two

"LET ME GET this straight. A gorgeous best man and an entire week at a first-class resort, where you can have tons of hot sex? Am I dreaming? Is this a dream?"

I have to give it to my editor. She knows how to encourage a girl's ideas.

"If I didn't know better, I'd think you'd talked Hayley into rigging the spinner, so I'd have to pick the best man." I'm in the process of trying desperately to close my stinking suitcase. It won't play nice.

"Oh, please. What, do you think your friend and I conspire against you?"

"You're the one who inspired her to make the darn spinner in the first place," I remind her. "Calling her behind my back like I'm a child in need of supervision. Why would I put conspiracy past you?"

"Well, to be honest, if I had known you were going away for a destination wedding, I would have certainly asked her to rig the device."

I burst out laughing.

"What?" she demands. "Kitty, one of us has to care about your career."

"Which implies I don't care. You're a piece of work."

Maggie sniffs like she's offended. "At any rate, who is this person? Have you learned anything about him? Is he even straight? This would all be a terrible waste of time if he wasn't."

I roll my eyes and mime putting a gun to my head. I'm alone in the apartment, so there's no one to see me do it, but still. I have to vent my frustration somehow, and something tells me that verbally unloading on my editor isn't the way to do it. "I don't think Hayley would be so dead set on me hooking up with him if there was doubt on that."

"Just the same, you'd do well to find out."

"What am I supposed to do? Flash him and see if he has a reaction? Or flat-out ask if he prefers men or women? For Pete's sake, you act like I grew up in a cave and just ventured out into the world yesterday."

"Fine. Take my advice as criticism."

Gee, here comes a headache. Why am I not surprised?

Maggie has a lot of terrific qualities, and I know she's fought for me more than once. I probably wouldn't have a career anymore if it wasn't for her going to bat for me against the company's executives when sales for my sweet romances started tanking.

But, I mean, how much am I supposed to take?

"I have everything under control," I assure her in a much more docile tone. "There's a bonus too. His family has a summer home in the Hamptons, where he always spends the season and commutes in and out of the city for work. So, if we hit it off, I'll have lots of atmosphere to work into the book. And I'll take plenty of pictures at the resort and post them all over social media too," I add as an afterthought.

"What a great idea."

I knew she'd like that.

"Get people talking about your next release before you've even started it. Of course, you'll start it soon. Right?"

"I'm packing my laptop," I promise with a sigh.

"Don't forget to have fun out there though. You need a little fun, and you deserve it. I'm not a complete ogre. I'm well aware of how hard you've been working."

How hard she's been working me, more like, but I'm not so frustrated with the packing process and her nitpicking to stir up another argument. No, I haven't enjoyed the pace at which I'm now working, and I sure didn't love it when she first told me I needed to spice things up and write "to trend."

But it's paying off. I can't deny that.

"And be safe, for heaven's sake," she adds before we get off the phone. "I don't want to read in the paper that a successful romance novelist was found dead on the beach or something."

"Oh my God."

"Well? It happens. Beautiful, young girls fall victim to wicked men all the time. There are men who prey upon tourists especially. It doesn't matter the exclusivity of the resort, Kitty. If anything, you're in more danger because of all the money surrounding you."

"Why don't I take a bath with my toaster right now and get it over with?"

"Take care and have fun!"

I swear, the woman swings from one mood to another quicker than I do. One second, I'm being murdered, and the next, I'm having fun.

There's a knock on the door around one in the afternoon while I'm still in the process of deciding what to cull from my suitcase if I'm ever going to get the darn thing shut without the zipper breaking and all my underwear exploding out.

"It's open!" I call out.

Yeah, I know. Not the safest thing to do, leaving my apartment unlocked. But I was expecting this.

"Where are you?" Matt's voice rings out from just inside before he closes the door.

Phoebe's quicker than he is. She finds me in my room and circles my legs.

"Smart girl." I give her lots of pets and belly scratches before looking up to find my neighbor with a bag full of what's sure to be delectable food in one hand.

"She smelled you, you realize that, right?" Always with the charm, this one.

"She's a smart girl anyway. It's not her fault she has you for an owner. I can't hold that one against her." Phoebe licks my hand. "See? She agrees with me."

"Woof. You're in a mood today. Are we eating lunch or what?" Only he doesn't follow when I brush past him to grab something to drink from the kitchen. "Still trying to pack?"

"Trying to unpack, actually. I don't have enough room in that big bag."

"The big bag." He snorts. "Along with the three smaller bags."

"What? We're going to be there for an entire week. A week full of activities, mind you. Hiking and boating and sightseeing. I'll need daytime outfits, nighttime outfits, bathing suits, something to wear to the rehearsal dinner, something for the wedding itself …"

"I get it; I get it. It sounds like a chore, this wedding." Matt goes to the living room and unpacks the bag, setting things on the coffee table like we usually do.

"Honestly, it sort of is, but I know Hayley would go nuts, being down there for an entire week with her family alone."

"She doesn't get along with them?"

"It's not that. They're all great people, but she's the least impressive of all three kids."

"I find that hard to believe!"

I sit across from him, cross-legged on the floor. Phoebe rests her chin on my knee, and I scratch her behind the ears. I'm going to be away for a week, so I need to get my pets and scratches in while I have the time.

"Kylie graduated college when she was nineteen and made COO of her firm by the time she was twenty-seven. Brandon is wicked smart and studying to be some sort of astrophysicist. She used to tease him about being a frat boy, but he's twenty-two now and anything but."

"Holy hell. No wonder Hayley is so driven."

"Can you imagine being as amazing as her and still only coming in third place? So, she gets the inevitable questions from extended family members who tease her about being the family slacker."

"That's the worst. Poor girl. No wonder she wants somebody there to keep her from drowning herself."

"Or drowning well-meaning family members."

"Though you do realize people are going to think you two are a couple because she brought you with her, right?"

"Please. Like I could land a smoke show like Hayley in my wildest dreams."

He chuckles, nodding. "You have a point."

"Oh, shut up. You weren't supposed to agree with me."

"You think I don't know that?"

"Anyway," I continue, raising my voice to speak

over him, "all is not lost. Yes, this is going to be a grueling week if we're expected to go on all these tours and hikes and whatnot, but there's a silver lining."

"The fact that you'll be at a five-star resort? For free?"

"Okay. Two silver linings."

"What's the other one?"

"My next trope is best man, thanks to Hayley being a sneaky little sneak, so I'll be taking inspiration for my next book while we're there."

He toys with his food, keeping his eyes averted, and I just know he's about to make a remark that's going to make me want to slug him. It never fails.

"What? What are you thinking?" I finally have to ask when I can't take it anymore.

"I wasn't thinking anything." He shrugs before popping a piece of chicken into his mouth and chewing a lot harder than he needs to.

"Lie."

"I wasn't."

"I mean, I know you don't think very much, Matt, but ..."

"It's just that I'm wondering when enough is enough."

"What do you mean?" I put my rice down on the table in case what he says next inspires me to throw the container at his head. I'm growing as a person.

"I mean, how many guys is Maggie gonna make

you date just to get another book out of you? It was funny at first; don't get me wrong."

"No duh. You laughed yourself sick how many times?"

"But now, it's been, what, almost a year? And you're still going out with one dude after another, all based on what they do for a living or whatever trope you're writing about this time. Isn't this all getting a little repetitive?"

"Well …"

"And don't even get me started on what it's got to be doing to you."

"To me?" I point to myself with my chopsticks. "What's that got to do with anything?"

His hazel eyes aren't sparkling when he hits me with a stony stare. "Come on. This is me you're talking to. Remember the time you came to my door, crying because you got dumped? Again."

"Wow. Way to remind me of a really crappy time in my life."

"You have to see what I mean though."

"I don't have to do anything." I can stare just as hard as he can, and I do.

We're practically a still life, except for the way Phoebe's tail occasionally smacks against the floor.

He blinks first. "Listen, I know why you had to do this in the first place. But don't you have enough, I don't know, experience now to write without having to date new men all the time? This is, what, your sixth book since you started the whole *dating by trope* thing?"

"Yes, it is."

"When does it all end? That's all I'm saying. I just want to understand. I don't like what Maggie's making you do. I've never liked it."

I have to take a deep breath. Okay, more than one deep breath. And while I'm at it, I remind myself how rude it would be to jam my chopsticks in his eye sockets.

If there's one simple shortcut to making me absolutely apoplectic with rage, it's telling me how I should and shouldn't feel about something. Making it out like I'm being manipulated. Like I have no say in my life.

"Maybe I like it." I shrug, taking pains to sound as blithe as I can. "It's a reason for me to get out and meet people. You know how reclusive I can be. This whole arrangement has forced me out of my comfort zone."

He only snorts before going back to his food. "Yeah, spin it that way."

"Ew, Matt."

"I'm calling it like I see it."

"You're making me sound like a slut, is what you're doing."

"No, I'm not saying that."

"Because I'm not."

"I know you aren't. I just don't want to see the big publisher use you to make a buck. I'm sorry for caring."

Now, he's all huffy, and I'm feeling rather huffy myself. We finish our lunch in silence before I shower Phoebe with a million kisses and promise to be back soon.

Though I have to wonder whether I'll be in a big hurry to see her owner once I get back.

How am I supposed to be friends with him when I know he thinks I'm so easily used?

Chapter Three

GRANDMOTHER WEARS AN approving little smile as she leans in to pour my tea. "When are you flying out?"

"First thing in the morning. We're going to the airport at four o'clock."

She winces. "I remember the days before this security heightening. You could dash to the airport, present your boarding pass, and be on the plane in moments. There was none of this waiting in line, removing one's shoes ..."

"You're showing your age." I wink.

"Laugh all you wish. There are times when I forget you're too young to remember what it was like before the world changed. I used to walk your grandfather to his gate when he was traveling, and I would meet him there when he returned."

"That's completely unthinkable now."

"I know that. As I said, times have changed. I can recall when there wasn't a single public place a person could visit without the certainty of reeking of smoke by the time they left." She lifts a shoulder while raising the teacup to her mouth. "Not everything has changed for the worse, come to think of it."

"Everybody must've stunk all the time."

"Yes, dear, but when everybody stinks, nobody minds very much."

Not exactly poetry, but I get what she's saying. "I'll have to write that into a book. It's a good line."

Instead of snickering or pretending she doesn't think I'm funny when I know she very well does, she frowns. "What's wrong?"

"Who says anything's wrong?"

"To start, twenty-five years of being your grandmother. I know we haven't always been close, but I have the instinct. And there is something troubling you."

Should I tell her? I want to tell her. In fact, I didn't know how much I wanted to tell her until just now, when she brought it up. I can't help it. What Matt said has been hanging over me like a shroud for hours.

"Do you think my publisher is using me?"

Her eyes widen. Gosh, they're so much like mine, the exact shade of blue. I hope to everything holy that by the time I reach her age, my skin is as smooth and radiant as hers. The woman has taken care of herself.

"Whatever made you ask that question?"

"Remember my neighbor Matt who you met at the auction? We don't always get along. Sort of like brothers and sisters, you know? Today, he gave me this big spiel about how my editor is using me, making me date all these different people just so I'll make more money for the company by writing more books."

She purses her crimson lips. I swear, I've never figured out the trick for making sure my lipstick doesn't bleed onto whatever I'm drinking from, but hers never budges. The woman's not even human.

"I see. And how did you feel when he offered this unsolicited opinion?"

She's good and mad. She knows how to hide it, but I know better. When her voice gets all clipped and tight, there's a storm brewing inside.

Knowing she sees how insulting he was gives me courage to keep talking. "Small. Weak. Manipulated. Like I have no say in my life. Like I'm something to be pitied."

"That is certainly not true."

"That's not how he made it sound."

"Men are a nuisance," she snaps.

"Pardon me, but having been a man since puberty, I take offense to that." Peter's smile is kind when he enters the room, and he pats me on the back in passing to show there aren't any hard feelings.

"I wasn't referring to you, dear." Her face practically glows.

I'm still giddy over seeing the two of them together after so many years of their relationship being strictly employer and employee. He's loved her and taken care of her for a very long time. Now, he gets to love her openly.

And she gets to love him.

He takes a seat next to her. "I hope you don't mind, but these big rooms tend to make a voice carry. I was on my way in when you spoke of your friend and his unwanted opinion."

"It's okay. I'm not trying to keep secrets." Besides, he's practically my grandfather. I wouldn't begrudge him anything, seeing how happy he makes my grandmother. "I just wish I could brush aside what he said and get on with things."

"What brought on the topic?" Grandmother asks.

"I'm going to try to meet and date the best man at the wedding."

"Oh. I see."

The two of them share a look.

"What? What did I say? Do you think that's wrong?"

"No, not at all. Though I would like to know who this young man is, if it's all the same to you."

Peter interjects before I have time to get snappy, "What I think concerns your grandmother is the notion that no matter who he is, you must date him because he's the best man. Not because he's a good man. Before, you had the opportunity to choose who you would get to know within that specific category. Now?"

"I see. Let me explain." I give them the quick-

and-dirty details of just how I ended up with this latest assignment, and by the time I'm finished, Grandmother's practically vibrating with anticipation.

"He's in finance *and* his family summers in the Hamptons?" I swear, the woman is about to swoon. "Oh, dear, that's a different story!"

"What? You wouldn't be okay with it if he was just some nobody from nowhere?"

Peter and I exchange looks, and I can't help but notice how crestfallen he's become. *Whoops*. I'd better change the subject—and fast. It has to be difficult for him, knowing she still carries at least a little bit of class snobbishness, no matter how she tells him it doesn't matter that he was her butler for so long.

"He's supposed to be a really nice person too," I add before she has the chance to put her foot in her mouth. "Hayley raved about him. I trust her judgment. She would never strong-arm me into dating a creep."

"That makes me feel a great deal better." Her hand closes over Peter's. "In the end, character is all that matters, naturally. I would always rather see you be happy, dear. Lord knows I've seen more than a few unhappy marriages in my sphere; I can tell you that much. Mercenary pairings, if you know what I mean. These never last. What truly matters are the feelings between the people involved."

He offers her a smile, though I can see what's

behind it. After all, it's only been a few months since he left for her sake, convinced he would be nothing but bad for her. What with them being members of two different social classes and all. It's ridiculous, and Grandmother was clearly heartbroken by it.

Since then, she's cut out anyone in her life who was mean or callous enough to give them a hard time for being together. I, for one, am not exactly weeping over the idea of never seeing some of her so-called friends again.

Still, Peter feels the difference even if she refuses to acknowledge it. Like when she makes little mistakes, encouraging me to date somebody just because his family's rich and he has a ritzy job.

"What do you both think about what Matt said?" It's easier to talk about that than about this Briggs person. I'm starting to wonder if he'll be worth the trouble I've already gone through, thanks to him.

Grandmother speaks up first, "I believe he needs to mind his own affairs. Frankly though, I can understand why he would be concerned. From a certain perspective, I can see how this looks problematic. I don't enjoy the notion of my granddaughter being used for the profit of a major publishing house. That CEO of yours makes millions, even billions, of dollars, and all because of people such as you. Doing the real work, sacrificing your personal life and your emotions so he can turn a profit."

That stings, especially since I happen to know the man she's referring to. He was the first person I dated for this little experiment after all. Blake Marlin is a billionaire, for sure, but he's not the fat cat she's making him out to be.

"Blake is a good man. He works too hard, but that's hardly a character flaw."

"You know what I mean, Kathryn. He profits from your work. I don't appreciate him putting you through this."

"You realize he's not the one doing it, right? He isn't making me do this. He's only the CEO of the company that owns a bunch of other companies. My publisher is just one of them."

"Dance around the truth all you'd like, granddaughter of mine, but that doesn't change a thing."

Peter, true to form, is much kinder. "How do you feel about it? What do you want out of your life and career, Kathryn?"

Wow. Sure didn't know I'd be getting roped into this discussion today. I guess I'm the only one to blame since I started the conversation flowing in this direction. "I'm not sure. I want to keep selling books—that I know. I want to be happy. I want the same sort of thing everybody else wants."

"Do you think this is the path to that future?"

Gosh, with the hard-hitting questions. "I mean, who can ever offer a definitive answer to that question? We can't look into the future. We can only make the best choices in the moment, right? And I'm not unhappy. That's the thing. I'm really not. I like my life."

"Then, by God, do what you want to do and tell anyone who feels otherwise where they can take their opinions." He chuckles slightly, a little sheepish. "Excuse me if I get a bit vocal when something matters as much as this."

My heart is so full; I can't even stand it. "I swear, if I thought I could compete with Grandmother for even a nanosecond, you'd both be in trouble." I lean over to kiss his cheek. "Thank you."

"Anytime." His eyes twinkle a little. "Though, please, do something for me."

"You know I would do anything for you."

"Be kind to that friend of yours. He cares about you; that much is clear. It isn't always easy for us to admit to the people we care for just how much we care. We might resort to judgment when there isn't any other way for us to demonstrate that caring."

Grandmother, of course, has an opinion of her own. "He needs to keep out of your business, that friend of yours. Perhaps he needs someone to remind him that not all opinions need voicing."

Peter pats her knee with a fond smile, and she softens. As always, they complement each other perfectly.

I wonder if I'll ever find the person who complements me that way.

"Do me one favor, dear," Grandmother adds as

I'm about to leave. "While you're at the resort, be sure to protect yourself."

"I'll wear plenty of sunscreen; don't worry."

"I didn't mean sunscreen, though you'd do well to steer clear of sunspots." She pats my cheek. "I meant, prophylactics. Condoms."

And that's what causes me to drop dead of embarrassment. The end.

Or so it seems as I leave Grandmother's and wish I could wipe the memory of her saying that from my brain for all time.

Chapter Four

"ARE YOU FLIPPING kidding me?" I have to take off my sunglasses when stepping out of the cab, which picked us up at the airport. Like it matters whether or not I'm looking around with sunglasses on.

There are times when a person needs to see things without a filter.

Like right now.

"Why are you surprised?" Hayley shakes her head at me, standing by my side. "We looked at pictures on the website. Remember?"

"Sure, but it's one thing to see something online and another to see it in front of you." Somehow, I manage to pry my eyes away from the sparkling jewel in front of me long enough to shoot her a look. "Don't tell me you don't think this is impressive."

"Oh, sure I do. I think it's fucking stunning." Spoken with Hayley's usual style. "But I'm not gonna stand around with my jaw touching the ground either. Besides, we're holding up the porter." She hands a few bills to our driver, who's on his way before I even think to thank him.

I would normally chafe at the way Hayley described me, but there's more than a little bit of truth to what she said.

I'm completely overwhelmed, and I know it looks that way.

But seriously, this place could be part of a movie set. In fact, I think I've seen it in more than one movie. The sort of place an extremely wealthy, connected, fabulous person stays.

The main building, which we sail into behind the porter pushing our luggage on a wheeled rack, is completely white from roof to foundation, making it shine under the bright sun. It's like a diamond nestled in blue velvet—that would be the sky, where not a single cloud is in sight.

From the moment we turned off the road, the fountains and palm trees lining both sides of the wide gravel drive leading to the main entrance told me this was going to be a special place. There are tropical flowers everywhere, and the aroma is enough to make me dizzy.

"Would you like a drink?" A young man in white linen approaches us as we wait at the concierge desk.

"I'll have a mai tai." Hayley turns to me, brows lifting.

"Just a water for me, thanks." When her brows lift even higher, I shrug. "I'm exhausted, and I know it would go straight to my head."

"Suit yourself, babe. As far as I'm concerned, we're on vacation."

Something tells me there's more to it than that, but I'm willing to bite my tongue. The way her eyes keep roaming the lobby is a dead giveaway.

She needs a drink to calm her nerves before any family members show up and ask if she's put on a little weight.

"You know, everybody's going to be so busy fawning over your sister this week, they won't even pay attention to you." I'm trying to be helpful. I really am. "You could probably streak through the resort and nobody would notice."

"How nice would that be for once?" She shoots me a grateful look. "You're a good friend."

"Who, me?" I point to myself with a shrug. "I'm just along for the ride."

Our waiter comes back with beverages around the same time we step up to the desk.

"Ah, yes, our wedding party. How was your trip?" The girl behind the desk is all smiles as she looks back and forth between us.

"Early," I groan, which earns me a giggle.

"You'll have plenty of opportunities to rest and relax now that you've arrived. We've included all the information you'll need here, in this folder." She hands it to me before turning away to the table running the length of the wall behind her.

I didn't notice them until now, too busy being glad we were finally there and staring in wonder at how beautiful everything is.

There's a long row of baskets sitting there, overflowing with items. The poor girl grunts softly as she picks one of them up; it's so heavy.

"Thank you for being part of our special day." Hayley lets out a soft sigh upon reading the handwritten note pinned to the basket. "Kylie's really outdone herself."

She has too. There's a bottle of wine with the names of the bride and groom printed on the label, two glasses, a candle, truffles, a little book titled *Our Love Story*, what I assume is an itinerary for the week, and more buried underneath.

"Wow. I'm ... impressed." I mean, there's being extra, and there's this. Not that I think I'd do much differently if this were my wedding.

Though let's be honest. I'd have to hire somebody to do it for me since I'd find a way to lose track of everything before I even got started.

"I have nothing but respect for anybody able to put something like this together."

We have to give the basket to the porter since it's too awkward for even the two of us to carry together. He puts it with the luggage and follows the concierge's instructions to find our room.

According to the map of the resort, the rooms are situated in various smaller buildings that sort of radiate from the main building in a half-circle. We step out of the main building and follow him down a flower-lined path to one of the outer longhouses.

"Ooh, there's somewhere I wanna visit." Hayley points to the pool, half-visible through even more thick, luscious flowers and palm trees.

"This is like heaven. Did we die and go to heaven?"

She laughs. "I doubt it. Though I'm sure Kylie would make up welcome baskets for that too."

"Don't be hard on her."

"She's a total social-media bride."

"Oh shoot!" I forgot about taking pictures for my accounts. Before we reach the longhouse, I manage to snap a few shots of pretty flowers and trees against that startling, ridiculous blue sky.

"Don't think so much about work."

"I find that hilarious, coming from you. You're the one who turned this trip into my working vacation, or did you forget?"

She's wearing sunglasses, but I know she's rolling her eyes. Call it a side effect of knowing somebody for a long time.

The rooms in the longhouse are positioned on either side of a long hallway.

"This is you, ladies." The porter opens the door, using an electronic key.

And I pretty much have to lean against the doorframe to keep from hitting the floor. "Holy. Cow."

I follow Hayley inside, and even she looks impressed. There are doors that open onto the beach. I mean, straight onto the beach with its white sand and blue-green water. We have a patio too. I can already imagine having breakfast out there.

Maybe while writing down my notes.

Talk about photo ops. I've always wanted to take one of those pictures where all you see is the person's feet and the view beyond. I can tag it, like, *Another day at the office.* Something cute like that.

Hayley tips the porter before he goes, leaving us alone. "Wow. I've gotta give it to my sister. This venue is amazing." She steps out onto the patio and takes a deep breath. "I could get used to this."

"Same here."

She grins back at me over her shoulder. "Has it ever occurred to you that you can work from anywhere in the world? Like, literally anywhere?"

"Yeah, I guess so."

"You could spend your whole life moving from place to place. A month here, a month there. I mean, it's not like you aren't paying an arm and a leg for that apartment. Hell, you could even sublet it and use that as income too." She spreads her arms. "This could be your home whenever you want it to be."

"It's tempting. But I don't know. I like having roots." I sit on the edge of one of the two beds and test its firmness—a mistake because, now, all I want to do is lie down. "Besides, I would miss you."

"I'd make the sacrifice of visiting whenever you wanted."

"You're such a generous person."

I need to get up since I might fall asleep if I don't, and there's way too much I want to see before the rest of Hayley's immediate family shows up and we're beholden to them.

"Oh my God, she made a book with little drawing versions of the two of them." Hayley flips through it, snickering. "Like anybody cares that he learned to make her favorite dinner to show how much he liked her. Is it that hard to make lasagna?"

Here I am, thinking it's sort of cute. But she's obviously in a mood just from being here and having it thrown in her face, how happy her successful sister is.

"You know my romance-writer's heart," I remind her with a slight laugh in hopes of keeping things light.

"You would think it's cute, wouldn't you?" She gives me a fake smile. "Sorry. I'm bitter."

"I wouldn't call it—"

"Bitter. I am. I admit it. I haven't even seen anybody from the family yet, and I'm already in a pissy mood. This isn't easy for me. Especially after ..."

She goes back to the book like it's the most important thing in the world. I know what she means, and I wish—not for the first time—that she'd told me about her affair with her boss while it was going on.

It seems like she caught real, true feelings for him. The jerk. He never deserved her.

"Looks like I should've ordered more than one drink," she murmurs with a wry grin, tucking the book into the basket.

"Probably not a good idea. You don't want to be so drunk that you end up saying things you'll regret."

"Wanna bet?"

"I know. Let's put our suits on and sit out by the pool. If you want a drink, let's have some atmosphere to go with it." I'm already digging through my carry-on, where I packed everything I'd need for a trip outside.

"Yeah, we should do that. But I should check in on my parents first. They've been here since last night, and if they find out I went to the pool before even saying hi ..."

"Got it. I'll grab us a table under an umbrella and wait for you there."

It only takes a few minutes to get changed and toss what I need into a tote bag. No matter what Hayley says, I'm not swanning around the pool in nothing but a bikini. My caftan is long and flowy and, in my opinion, dramatic. It's the sort of thing a romance writer would wear poolside.

Obviously, since I'm going to wear it poolside.

It's only around eleven in the morning by the time I take a seat at a table, but there are already at least two dozen people out and about. Bronzed, beautiful people.

It's enough for the time being to take a few photos and schedule them to post across my accounts later. One of the pool, which is crystal clear and inviting on a warm day. One of the beach beyond. I'll have to take plenty of shots from the patio, for sure.

"Maggie's gonna love this," I murmur with a smile while typing up captions for each image.

"Can I get you a drink, miss?"

I smile up at the server and decide on something that comes in a pineapple. Another great, if somewhat cliché, image. But Maggie's sort of cliché anyway, and she's really the person I'm doing this to please. Sure, my fans will like it, but they won't hound me the way she will.

"Are you fucking kidding me?"

It's delivered in such a sharp, nasty tone that I can't help but look up and around to see who said it.

A guy is pacing back and forth on a path leading to the pool. He's scrubbing a hand through his hair, to the point where it's sticking up in blond spikes. He's talking on a phone.

Yelling into a phone, more like it.

"You had weeks to tell me that. Weeks. How do you think this is going to look? What do you mean, you don't care? I already paid for everything! Do you even know what this is costing me? Do you think I have all this money to throw around? Yeah, he's paying for me, but I was paying for you. What difference does it make? You could've at least gotten a free vacation out of it."

He lets out a bark of a laugh. "You? Not wanting something for free? Since when? Fucking hell."

By now, there are people eyeing him up with disgust. It's not a pretty sight or sound, watching and listening to a full-grown man having a meltdown.

"Fuck off, Linds." He shoves the phone into his pocket before letting out a few more choice words at a significant volume.

Which, of course, is when I have to say something. "Hey. There are other people in the world besides you. You're being rude."

That leaves a few people snickering and nodding in agreement, which gives me more courage.

It also earns me an absolutely filthy look from him.

"Was I talking to you?"

"I don't know. Were you? You were practically screaming, so, yeah, you could've been talking to me."

"Mind your business."

"Keep your business to yourself, and I'll mind mine. How about it?"

He's halfway to the table by the time I realize I've really done it. Why not dance a jig in the middle of a minefield? I don't know this man from Adam, yet I've gone and made him mad.

And he's on his way over to me.

Until Hayley intercepts him.

"Briggs! Just the person I wanted to see!" She hurries over and gives him a hug around the neck. "Thank God there's somebody else here who I can actually stand to spend more than a minute at a time with!"

Briggs.

This is Briggs.

Also known as the best man. Also known as the guy I'm supposed to meet, form a connection with, and, if Maggie has her way, engage in sweaty, rum-fueled sex with.

The guy who looks like he would gladly strangle me once he's finished strangling the girl he just screamed at over the phone.

Of.

Freaking.

Course.

Chapter Five

IT'S CLEAR HAYLEY has no idea what she missed just before she got to the pool.

She has no idea the super-nice, awesome, friendly guy she's so sure I'll hit it off with is basically a jerk with no sense of how to behave himself in public.

"Come on. Have a seat with us! I've been dying to introduce you to my best friend. I think I mentioned her to you over Christmas, when we met up at the party. Do you remember?"

Briggs looks dazed, but then he would now that Hurricane Hayley has taken control of the situation. Now that she's here, he's a different person. The man she thinks he is.

"Yeah, now that you mention it, I do remember you talking about a friend who's a writer." He looks me up and down with eyes roughly the color of the water in the pool.

It's a shame he's got those eyes and that golden hair and a jaw sharp enough to cut glass.

Because he's repulsive on the inside.

"Kellen Briggs." He holds a hand out to shake,

giving me a look that says I'd better play along for the time being.

So, I do. "Kitty Valentine. So, your name is Kellen. Hayley couldn't remember when I asked."

She laughs, of course, though it's a little tight. A little forced. I'm not playing as nice as she wishes I would, but then she has no idea what I witnessed from this dude.

"Yeah, all my life. There were three Kellens in our friend group in school, so everybody started calling me by my last name and then shortened it." He sits across from me with Hayley at my right since there was no chance of him getting away. Not with her tugging his arm the way she was.

"So, how's it going? What have you been up to?" she asks.

I raise an eyebrow, watching him. Yes, what has he been up to?

"Not much lately. Work. You know how it is. So, she's your date for the wedding?"

"Yep. She's my plus-one," Hayley explains. "Single as they come."

Oh, thank you so much, Hayley.

"I see." He smirks a little. "Me too."

"I can't imagine why."

Hayley shoots me a look of unadulterated horror. Sure, anybody who doesn't know me might've taken that at face value. Because, at face value, the guy's a catch. Handsome, probably successful in his work. Everything that makes somebody attractive on paper.

But she knows me, and she knows how I sound when I'm being sarcastic.

He smirks even more than before. "I invited a girl I was casually dating for a while. She seemed excited about coming but never showed up for the flight today."

Once again, I can't imagine why.

Hayley's face falls. "Oh, that sucks. Well, it's her loss. And, hey"—she looks at me and then back at him—"with me being busy with family stuff all week, maybe you and Kitty could spend time together. I know I won't get out of at least one family dinner—and no offense, Kitty, but I think it's just parents and kids."

She's so full of it. I have to kick her a little under the table. Her parents are amazing, and they'd never tell me not to come to dinner.

But she's working overtime to get me and Mr. Foul Mouth to spend one-on-one time together.

"I don't know." Kellen shrugs. "I might have a bunch of best-man stuff to do."

"I know the job must be difficult."

This time, Hayley kicks me. I kick out again, but she moves her leg out of the way in time.

"I'm gonna get a drink," she announces. "Do either of you want one?"

"I'm still good on this one." I hold up my pineapple, which is half-full and quite delicious.

"I'm okay." Kellen's smile drops off his face the

second he's out of Hayley's line of sight. He glowers at me from across the table while she waves her arms behind him and mimes smiling and being friendly.

I cannot stand her right now.

"So what was that all about?"

"She's just trying to help me meet a man."

"Help you? What, are you desperate? Can you not find a man on your own?"

I have to swallow back the rush of absolute indignation at this. If he were Matt, I would've thrown something at him by now. The creep.

I might still throw something. Anybody who heard that little exchange on the phone would understand why.

"You know I'm a writer. I'm supposed to write about dating a best man for my next book. It was her idea. She thought we would—"

"So, what?" he asks because, apparently, I'm not allowed to finish a sentence without him interrupting me. "You write memoirs? Based on what you do?"

"No. Romance novels. Fiction based in reality."

"You don't have an imagination?" He taps a finger to his head. "You can't make things up? I thought that was what writers did."

"They do. It's a long story, and I don't feel like explaining myself to you when you're so obviously determined to be a jerk."

"You're the one who got mouthy before."

"Mouthy?" I laugh. "That is so something I'd expect to hear you say. I bet you don't like it much when women get mouthy, do you? And I bet they get mouthy on you a lot. Whenever one of them says something you don't like, they're mouthy."

"You don't know the first thing about me."

"Don't I? I heard enough from you before. Maybe if you'd kept your conversation private instead of yelling in front of the whole pool—"

"I didn't know she was going to call when she did—"

"If you interrupt me one more time, I swear, you'll end up with bits of pineapple all over you. Try me if you think I'm kidding."

He rolls his eyes but keeps his mouth shut this time.

"You came off like a bully. And the way you stormed over here was the way a bully would storm over. I'm sorry if you don't like my perception, but that's how it was."

He sighs, staring at the table with his lips pursed. "I'm not usually like that. I do apologize for coming off that way. Nobody wants to be told they're acting like a jackass when they're already mad enough to kill somebody." His eyes dart up to meet mine before flickering away again. "Just a turn of phrase. Not literal."

"You were talking to the girl who was supposed to come with you?"

"She's a gold digger. Hot, fun to be with, but a

gold digger. Not that I have that much gold. But she got all excited when I offered to bring her with me. Let me pay for it. Kept me thinking she was coming along, even when I reminded her the refund period was coming to a close. Didn't tell me she never planned on actually showing up at the airport."

He shrugs. "Oldest story in the world. She's dating somebody else. Not that we were ever serious. It was one of those things. We'd meet up, remember why we liked each other. Though who knows? She could've been cheating on her boyfriend with me, and I wouldn't have known it. I doubt I'd ever get a straight answer out of her."

"I see. Well, I'm sorry, for what it's worth."

"Thanks. For what it's worth." But he smiles for a split second.

He then looks around, and I follow his gaze, realizing Hayley is not at the bar.

"Where's Hayley?" he asks.

"Oh, she's not coming back. Knowing her, it's her way of making sure we're together with nothing to do but get to know each other."

"I see."

"She actually rigged it, so I'd end up writing about a best man for my next book." He looks hopelessly confused. "Like I said, long story," I add.

His mouth twitches, his eyes crinkling a little at the corners, hinting at him maybe having a decent personality when he's not in the middle of getting stood up by a girl and making a scene. "So, she's determined to get us together during this whole thing, huh?"

"She's a determined sort of person. She once convinced me to get bangs. It was not a good look for me, but she'd talked me into it."

"That's pretty persuasive." He's fighting back a grin now.

"Yeah, she'll kill it in the courtroom. Nobody will have a chance against her."

"Look"—he finally relaxes, his shoulders lowering to a regular height instead of being up around his ears—"I'm not the guy you met back there. Really, I'm not. I let my anger get the better of me, and I shouldn't have. Especially out in public. I really am sorry for how I acted."

I mean, I did threaten to throw pineapple at him. "I understand. I saw you at your worst—at least, I hope that was your worst."

"You've never seen me when my college bracket falls apart."

"Ugh, you like college basketball?" I wrinkle my nose and roll my eyes. "No way we can even be friends."

"I played back at school. I was on a basketball scholarship actually."

"No kidding. Couldn't cut the pros?"

"Oof." He winces. "Low blow. Actually, I blew my ACL and just wasn't the same after that."

"Oh. I'm sorry. I shouldn't have joked."

"It's okay. I wasn't pro material. And I'm good

with money and numbers, so …"

"So, it worked out the way it was meant to work out."

"Seems that way. I guess everything does. Either that or it's what we tell ourselves to make up for having no control over our existence."

Hmm. He's an interesting person. A little dark maybe. A pessimist. I'm hardly a ray of sunshine most of the time myself.

But he's smart. I have to give him that.

And gorgeous—when he isn't ready to strangle somebody.

Though I'm still not completely sure about him. Whether we'll be a fit or not. But I can at least get to know him better over the week. It seems like we'll get along fairly well.

"Do you really have a ton of best-man things to do this week?" I have to ask.

"Nah. We'll drink the night before the wedding, but that's it. We already had the bachelor party—what there was of it. Zack didn't wanna do anything he'd end up feeling guilty over." He chuckles. "A few of the guys were disappointed. Zack told them to get lives. They told him to stop being so p—I mean, so whipped."

I know what he was about to say and appreciate that he held back. Okay, so he's a decent enough guy. "How did you feel about it?"

"I didn't care. We played pool and drank scotch and went back to my place to watch a game. I'm fine with that. I got all the partying out of my system back in school."

I'll have to keep an eye on him this week and see if that's really true. It's all well and good for a person to pretend like they don't party.

But a guy like him? On an island resort? With bridesmaids probably ready to fall into his bed?

We'll see.

"If you want," he offers, "maybe we could grab dinner whenever Hayley's busy with the family. Knowing Kylie, she'll have her jumping through hoops and opening doors and pulling out chairs for her."

"I'd love to see her try," I admit with a laugh. "Nobody gets Hayley to do anything she doesn't feel like doing."

"Then, you've never seen Kylie in action. Don't get me wrong; she's a great girl, and I think she's perfect for Zack. But she's Type A if there ever was one. And this is her show." He spreads his arms in a shrug. "We're just the supporting cast."

"I hope you know I'm going to use that line in a book someday."

He winks with a killer smile that lights up his whole face and makes him handsomer than ever. "So long as I get a cut of the royalties and a glowing thank-you in the notes."

Chapter Six

"SO, YOU'RE THE famous Kitty Valentine." Hayley's godmother gives me the once-over without bothering to make it look like she's doing anything else.

All I can do is shrug with a goofy smile since what's a girl supposed to do when she hears that? She made it sound like there'd been reports of me, like killing and eating men foolish enough to wander into my den.

"That's me. I guess it's better than having you call me infamous," I offer.

She sniffs, swirling her wine. "I was going to but thought it would be rude."

Oh. Well then.

She smiles in a way that reminds me of Grandmother's so-called friends. I wonder if the two of them have ever crossed paths.

"Hayley raves about you all the time," she explains. "She's very proud."

"I'm proud of her too. She's going to have an amazing career."

"I am certain she will, though I wonder if she'll ever manage to eclipse her brother and sister." She raises her glass of wine in Kylie's direction.

Kylie gives her a distracted smile. I hope the girl will be able to enjoy her own wedding at this rate. She's wound so tight. Will she even remember any of this, or will it be nothing more than a few brief flashes of memory and a lot of disappointment at her plans not going right?

I really hope that's not the case.

Rather than remind Hayley's godmother that there shouldn't be any competition between Hayley and her siblings, I manage to make an escape.

I can see why Hayley wasn't looking forward to tonight. Actually, I can see why she wasn't looking forward to coming on this trip.

Not that it isn't nice. Not that Kylie and her bridesmaids didn't put a ton of work into it.

It's just feels so … forced. Like, manufactured fun.

Kylie taps a fork against her wineglass, signaling for us to be quiet. I'm waiting at the bar in the small banquet room while everybody else mingles.

"Thank you all so much for being here. We know it's not easy to take time out of your busy schedules to celebrate with us this way, and it means the world. It truly does." She mimes applauding all of us, and most of the room follows suit.

I don't. I mean, I'm not family, and I get the feeling she isn't talking to me. Not that she'd be rude, but I'm just a guest. Practically a freeloader really.

My gaze travels over the room, and I notice Kellen isn't smiling or clapping either.

He's looking at me.

Granted, I wish he were smiling, but still. It seems like we're of the same mind on this.

"Everybody, have a nice time tonight, but don't stay up too late," Kylie urges. "We have so much planned this week; you'll need every ounce of energy if you want to keep up."

Kellen joins me a moment later. "Gee, I sure do want to keep up."

I have to hide a giggle, both because I don't want anybody to think I'm laughing at Kylie and because he doesn't need to know yet that I think he's funny. Let him work for my laughter, I say.

"Have you seen the itinerary?" he murmurs while signaling for a drink.

He looks good. Smells good too. Good enough that I can't resist the urge to joke with him a little.

So, I lift a shoulder. "You mean, the schedule of events that happens to be completely up to us whether we want to join or not, but we all know there's no option?"

He chuckles. "I thought you seemed like you might be cool, if given the chance."

"Wow. That's a backhanded compliment if ever I heard one. I'm cool all the time."

"Really?" He fixes me with a wry look from under his brows.

"Okay, okay, I'm a total nerd. If Hayley ever talked about me, I'm sure she could confirm that."

"She already did. Ages ago. Her friend Kitty, the nerdy writer."

"She would never say that."

"So you would think." He's laughing as he looks around the room. "I swear, if Kylie makes it to the wedding without the top of her head blowing off, it'll be a miracle. At least this place is nice."

"It's very nice. And you should know how nice since you paid for somebody else to join you."

He covers his chest with one hand like I wounded him. "Ouch! Damn, you're tough."

"That was a risk," I admit. "I didn't know how you'd take it. I guess the wine has me feeling more confident. Or snarky. Either way."

"I guess I have a thing for snark since that should've pissed me off, but it only makes me kinda like you. I lift an eyebrow. "I said kinda," he adds.

"You like snark? I can give you snark. I can snark along with the best of them. All day long."

"Okay, there's a limit."

"Suit yourself." I shrug.

"At least there's somebody else here who sees this the way I do. Between you and me …"

He leans in a little closer, though he doesn't strictly need to. There isn't a ton of noise in here, and I can hear him clearly.

I don't mind.

He smiles before backing away toward where

Zack and a couple of the groomsmen are doing shots. "I'm glad there's somebody I can relate to. Somebody who isn't a giggly airhead."

And I'm glad his would-be guest never showed.

Maybe Hayley was onto something. *Why does she always have to be right?*

I excuse myself and find her in a corner, talking with her brother. Brandon is pretty much the male version of his sisters—gorgeous and blond with a dazzling smile and perfect bone structure.

He's prettier than me, in other words.

I'd hate him if he wasn't such a nice guy.

"Hey!" he greets me with a big, tight hug. "How are you? It's been so long."

"I know, right? My editor pretty much keeps me chained to my desk most of the time."

"I try to get her out into the world every once in a while," Hayley tells him, elbowing me.

"Yeah, but she's not much better. Always working."

"You were made for each other." He blows out a sigh, his cheeks puffing out. "This is really something, isn't it?"

I can tell he's trying to be generous. He doesn't seem all that interested in appearances.

"It is. I think it's very, very nice," I whisper in a chiding way. "Don't give Kylie a hard time. This is her dream. She deserves it. Every girl does."

"Spoken like a true romantic." He kisses the top of my head and then winks. "I need alcohol."

We watch him walk away, and for Hayley's benefit, I let out a low whistle. "I swear, if he wasn't your brother …"

"Watch your mouth, woman."

"He's hot. Your brother is certifiably hot. Get used to it."

"I refuse to hear this." Then, she nudges me. "What about Briggs, huh?"

"Can we please refer to him as Kellen? I refuse to use his last name if I'm supposed to take him seriously as a human being."

"If you walk around, calling him Kellen, nobody's going to know who you're talking about."

"Fine, I'll call him Briggs when we're exchanging vows someday, just so nobody's confused."

It's good to see and hear her genuinely laugh even if it's sort of at my expense. "Kitty Briggs. I don't like it."

"I'll always be Kitty Valentine. It's my brand."

"Damn straight. Besides, yelling at you and reminding you you're Kitty fucking Briggs doesn't have the same ring to it."

I have to shush her since, hello, there are people around who know who she's talking about. "Okay, let's not get any rumors started. It's bad enough he knows why you wanted us to hook up in the first place."

"Which you didn't have to tell him."

"I needed to tell him something. We didn't exactly get off to the best start, you know. It was the icebreaker. After what I heard from him earlier, if I wrote about him without him knowing, I'd half-expect him to accuse me of trying to steal from his life or something."

"He wouldn't do that."

"I didn't know that at the time. Heck, I still don't. You never know how a person's going to react in a situation like that. No matter how nice they are."

"He keeps looking at you." I start to look around. "Don't!" she hisses, squeezing my arm. "You don't look when a person tells you that. Jeez, it's like I've taught you nothing."

"What do you expect me to do when you tell me somebody's looking at me?"

"Let out a sparkling laugh, like life is so amazing and wonderful and you're so funny. Obviously."

"If I'd laughed, it would've meant you said something funny. Dork." I give her wineglass a pointed look. "Are you sure you haven't had too much?"

"Mind your business." She finishes the glass and hands it off to a passing server in one single, smooth move. Even now, stressed out and already tired of being compared to her siblings and slightly tipsy, she makes everything look so effortless.

"Okay, fine." Her parents catch my eye from across the room, and I offer them a smile. "Your folks seem happy."

"They are. Their shining star is getting married."

I put an arm around her. "You're a shining star too. You eclipse me, for sure."

She rolls her eyes. "That's different."

"Why, because I'm such a nerd?"

"Something like that." She's smiling again, which is good. "But thanks. I'm glad you're here. In case I forget to say it while I'm in the middle of bridesmaid hell, I figured I should say it now."

"I'm glad too. You need somebody here to keep you sane. I'm happy it's me."

Kylie waves Hayley over from across the room, where everybody is posing for pictures.

"I never thought you'd be the one keeping me sane, but here we are."

"Yeah, life's funny like that." I give her a tiny shove in her family's direction and watch with a whole lot of sympathy as her mother arranges her hair, which looked pretty the way it was.

There was a time when I wondered what drove Hayley. What made her work so hard.

Then, I spent about five minutes around her family and never had to ask that question again.

She catches my eye, and I wince in sympathy, standing alone. Like the outsider I am. Which is okay since it gives me ample ability to observe. The way a writer does.

Except I'm not the only one observing.

I feel eyes on me. I know it's probably no more than paranoia—*who'd be watching me right now when there's a bride and her bridesmaids? And, hey, let's not even talk about the scenery*—but I can't shake the feeling. Somebody's watching me.

Should I laugh like I just said something sparklingly witty?

Uh, no, since I'm standing alone, I don't think laughter would have the intended effect.

Despite Hayley's advice, I take a look around. Casual-like. No big deal.

And I find a pair of turquoise eyes looking back at me.

Only Kellen isn't like most people. He won't look away, embarrassed at getting caught.

If anything, he holds my gaze. Daring me to react. To avert my eyes.

I have to eventually, moving across the room to tease Brandon about the bridesmaids who are clearly sizing him up like they want to share him for dessert.

And I tell myself the flush on my cheeks has to do with getting too much sun this morning.

Chapter Seven

"THERE ISN'T ENOUGH coffee in the whole wide world." I respond to Hayley's groans with a groan of my own. Funny how the sparkle has already dimmed with the two of us stumbling from our room in time to meet with the group before going on our bus tour of the mountains.

This resort seemed so magical yesterday.

After I didn't get enough sleep for the second night in a row, it feels a little too sunny and shiny. But there was no way anyone was leaving the party last night.

My feet are dragging across the gravel pathways, and I'm not so jazzed about exotic flowers anymore. Like, who do they think they are, all colorful and fragrant and whatnot?

"Do I have to?" I must've asked that question ten times by now, like a toddler.

"Yes." When Hayley starts with the one-worded answers, I know she's good and tired.

Does that stop me from pestering her? Of course not.

"But I'm not even part of the bridal party."

"So help me," she hisses. From the squint lines on her face I can tell she's glaring at me from behind her sunglasses.

"I'm just saying."

"And I'm just saying, enough already. You're here as my guest, and I refuse to go through this alone. If I don't show, it's a whole thing. I don't want this to be a whole thing." She turns her head to glare at me again just before we enter the main building. "And neither do you, Kathryn Antoinette."

Oh. So, that's how it is. The gloves have come off.

I'd tell her she owes me for this, but I'm not entirely out of my mind. The girl has made it possible for me to enjoy a week in paradise.

If paradise were chock-full of forced group activities. I mean, there's a reason I'm a writer, and it's not because I work well in groups.

Still, I put on a happy face when we find the rest of our group waiting by the front desk like dutiful soldiers.

Bleary-eyed, hungover, dutiful soldiers. I'm so glad I slowed down my drinking last night. It looks like the groomsmen are leaning on the desk to keep from falling over.

Except for one of them. Of course, he catches my attention first and foremost. It's one of those psychological things. You tell yourself not to think about something or somebody and that's the only thing on your mind.

He looks good—like, not just good compared to the testaments to binge-drinking who surround him. The man might've just gotten back from a trip to the spa. He's rested, refreshed, wearing a bright polo shirt that makes his eyes pop.

Not that they need any help doing that.

Kylie's smile shows off just about all her teeth. "Great! Now that we're all here, we can get started."

"Wow. Be a little more obvious," Hayley mutters under her breath.

I don't bother chiding her because I just got scolded in the most passive-aggressive way possible.

There's nothing that makes my skin crawl more than being spoken to like I'm a naughty little girl. I have to briefly wonder how Kylie would look on her big day with a black eye.

Lack of sleep does wonders for my mood, I think sarcastically to myself.

"The bus is waiting outside." Kylie is all mother duck, gathering her ducklings and moving us toward the door.

I pick up a pair of iced coffees from a tray. I guess there were more earlier along with a continental breakfast. There are still muffins and pastries available.

"Here." I hand Hayley the coffees before sliding a few pastries into my purse and then a couple muffins into hers.

"We definitely look like the low-class guests right now," she whispers, handing me back my coffee.

"I don't see you refusing the food. Sorry that I don't feel like going hungry this morning."

This early, early morning. It's not even seven o'clock, but here we are, boarding a bus. Would it help if I begged a random passerby to rescue me? Too late. We're getting on the bus, the last two in line.

"I need you to be on time for things," Kylie whispers in a fierce tone when Hayley reaches her.

"I need you to schedule things at a decent hour," Hayley fires back—and she doesn't bother whispering.

There are a few snickers from others in the vicinity, though I notice their expressions go blank and innocent the second Kylie looks around to find the culprits.

I feel sorry for her. I do. I only suspected she couldn't possibly enjoy this when I first got here and saw how she was acting. Now? I'm absolutely sure of it. No way is she having a good time.

It seems wrong.

But I can't exactly sit and have a heart-to-heart with her now. Especially when the bus is moving and, as everybody knows, we held up the departure.

"I have a seat free." Kellen waves to Hayley and me as we make our way down the row, swaying back and forth and clutching the seats to keep from falling.

"I'll keep going. I think my brother needs help."

Darn her.

It doesn't matter that Hayley's half-dead from exhaustion; she's still working on getting me hooked up. She gives us both a little grin, nodding toward the back. Sure enough, two girls are flirting with Brandon, and the poor guy is not going to be happy with his sister's interference.

Kellen snorts. "Brandon's smart and good with the ladies."

"So you know him?" I look over my shoulder in time to see him shoot Hayley an annoyed look.

"I know he seemed pretty comfortable with you last night."

I throw him a *Look*. Capital *L* included. "Why were you paying attention in the first place?"

"What else was there to pay attention to?" He shrugs like it doesn't matter.

For the second time, I'm asking myself why he doesn't respond to things the way other people do. He didn't look away when I saw him watching me.

And he doesn't even have the decency to act embarrassed now that I've caught him admitting he was paying close attention.

Maybe he didn't think there was anything to be embarrassed about?

"Brandon's comfortable with me because he knows me." I shrug it off. "That's not the same as getting relentlessly hit on by strangers who could take advantage of him."

"You're protective of him." It's not a question.

"He's the little brother I never had and I want the best for him."

"He's a grown man."

"He is. He's also super smart, possibly a little naive, and has gotten too hot for his own good. I don't want him to get taken advantage of. Those girls will chew him up and spit him out."

"So you've taken it upon yourself to look out for him."

Another *Look.* "Never mind. I think I'm going to find another seat."

He reaches out, taking my wrist in a gentle grip. "Sorry, sorry. I think you're just not understanding my sense of humor."

"Sense of humor?" I roll my eyes. "That wasn't humor. You were being mean."

"I wasn't trying to. I actually think it's sort of nice. And I keep forgetting you're a sincere person."

"Is there anything wrong with that?"

"No. It's odd, yeah, but that's not your fault." He chuckles, leaning back in the seat with a sigh. "I'm jaded. A born cynic. I don't find it easy to believe the best about people right away."

"That … sucks."

"You're also pretty blunt." He grins.

"It must suck though. I didn't say you sucked. Just that the situation sucks. Not being able to believe good things about people right away, like everybody has an ulterior motive."

"A lot of people do."

"A lot of people don't."

He frowns. "Where did you grow up? Somewhere over the rainbow?"

"No. Brooklyn."

"Okay, so not over the rainbow."

"Hardly. Nobody would ever mistake me for a Pollyanna. I'm fairly cynical myself, but I don't believe the worst about people as soon as I meet them."

He nods slowly, eyes narrowing. "Yeah. I guess you have to have that kind of outlook if you're gonna write romance. You can't be a jaded asshole like me."

"Wow. Are you sure you shouldn't go into sales? Because you're so good at selling yourself."

He chuckles. "That's me. The consummate salesman. I guess an early wake-up time wasn't helpful either. I've been in a better mood."

"Oh, don't get me started." I can barely stifle a yawn. "I think Hayley might've drowned me in the pool if I asked one more time whether I really had to do this."

"I'm the best man, so I didn't have a choice either way."

I have to laugh. "Yeah, and it's cute that you think I had a choice."

He glances out the window to his left before

jerking a thumb out there. "We're missing all this scenery, you know."

The scenery sitting next to me is much more interesting, but he has a point. We're supposed to be looking around, taking it in.

Jeez, do I wish I hadn't looked.

"What's wrong?" He's stunned, judging by the way his voice breaks a little when my nails dig into his arm.

I have to hide my face in his shoulder. "We're up so high!"

"Yeah. It's a mountain."

"Oh my God." I close my eyes, teeth clenched. "Why are we so close to the side of the road?"

"Because this is the road. Kitty, breathe." His voice is gentle. He pats my arm. "You're scared of heights?"

"I live in Manhattan. Heights aren't a problem. Being on a road without a rail along the side, hundreds of feet up? That's the problem."

He pats my arm again. "Okay. Just breathe. Talk to me. Tell me stuff about you."

"Like what?"

"Like how your hands got so strong."

He surprises me into laughing a little. I can't bear the thought of opening my eyes, but the tightness in my chest loosens enough that I can speak without squeaking.

"I type for a living, remember?"

"Oh, right. How many books have you published?"

"A lot. I don't know." I honestly don't. I can't even think. My insides feel tight and fluttery in a sickening way.

"Okay. What's your favorite part about writing?"

His voice is low, his mouth close to my ear. While I'm half out of my mind with terror, it registers how nice he's being.

"Making my own happy endings."

The sound of his breath catching isn't lost on me, even now.

"It's the truth," I add when he doesn't say anything for a while.

"I know. It's just not what I expected you to say."

"How do you know what to expect from me when we don't know each other?"

A brief snicker. "Remember, I'm a cynical asshole."

The bus comes to a stop.

"Tell me we're where we were supposed to end up and this isn't a brief pause," I whisper.

"We're where we were supposed to end up. We'll be on our way back down after everybody gets off to take pictures." There's a sharp intake of breath. "Kitty. The claws."

Right. My nails are practically breaking the skin. If I were in a decent state of mind, I might even give him credit for his turn of phrase. Instead, I force my fingers to loosen. "Sorry. Please tell me I don't have to go out there."

"You don't have to go out there."

"Will you stay with me?"

"I'll stay with you."

And he does. While everybody goes out to look at the view and take pictures, he sits with me the entire time.

Chapter Eight

"WHAT HAPPENED THEN?"

"Nothing." I shrug, staring at the water. It's easier than looking even my best friend in the eye.

I'm still so embarrassed over what happened on the bus. How I lost it. "I swear, I had no idea I was going to freak out that way. I didn't even give it a moment's thought, you know? A bus tour. No biggie."

"I know. It's okay. These things happen to everybody. You don't know something's going to freak you out until you're in the situation and there's nothing you can do about it."

"It's not like I could walk down the mountain."

"Exactly. You were trapped."

Still, there's something in her voice that makes me nudge her. We're sitting on the beach, stretched out on lounge chairs. Finally relaxing for the first time since we got here.

Though there's no such thing as taking a vacation from scrutiny.

"What? What aren't you asking?"

She purses her lips. "I was only wondering what

you two talked about. What happened when you were alone on the bus."

"Ew!"

"What?" She's laughing, teasing me.

"Hayley, I thought I was going to die. I've never felt that way before, that sort of panic attack. My heart was racing, and my stomach was in knots. I could hardly breathe or think."

"Except for the stomach part, that sounds like it could be the result of something else …"

"You're the absolute worst. Trust me, the only thing on my mind was getting off the mountain without dying. He was nice to stay with me."

"He was very nice. I'm not arguing that. It was cool of him to talk to you. I'm assuming he talked to you."

"The whole time."

"About what?"

"Gosh, I can barely remember. It was all a way to take my mind off things." With my hands over my face, I groan. "Everybody has to think I'm a complete idiot. I know they were all looking at me funny and whispering about me."

"Not everybody."

"Is that supposed to make me feel better?"

"I hoped it would." She lowers her sunglasses, eyeing me. "I mean, some of these girls are total bitches. I hate even being associated with them through this wedding and can't wait to never see them again. Though I guess they'll be at the baby shower someday, if Kylie ever has a kid."

"Why does she have so many bridesmaids? I mean, eight seems a little much."

"Because she has soooo many friends." Hayley snorts before leaning back in her chair. "It's a shame they're all wretched."

"She seems smarter than them. Too smart to want to spend time with them."

"They were sorority sisters. Honestly? I think she was so grateful to be accepted by older girls. With her going into college so early and everything, she wasn't exactly popular. Most of the people there thought of her as a freak, I think."

"Jeez." I never considered that before. It had to be lonely for her.

"But they welcomed her into the sorority, and I know she felt privileged to be in their company. I can't imagine it personally since they're the worst. But I'm older now than she was then, so it's easier for me to see. Now, I think she sticks with them out of habit and feels like she has to. Besides, she's so busy with work all the time; she doesn't have the energy to make new friends."

I never expected a whole dissertation. "Not that you've given any thought to this."

"Shut it."

"No, it's okay. You're her sister. It's only natural for you to have given this some thought. Especially when you don't like those girls. You must've done a lot of wondering about why she spends time with them."

"Yeah. Among other things she's made me wonder about."

"Speak of the devil." I jerk my head slightly, indicating the group of girls farther down the beach. Kylie is with them. "I hope she finally chills out. Maybe a couple fruity drinks will help."

"I don't know that drinks will take the stick out of her ass."

"I think I feel sorry for her."

"You would."

"I'm just saying. I love you. You know I do. But it's not like she tied you up and held lit matches to your feet. Imagine peaking at a super-early age. You have to spend the rest of your life living up to that impossible standard."

"Sounds a little like you."

"Oof, you nasty thing."

"I wasn't trying to be nasty. Seriously, I wasn't," she insists. "I'm saying, it really does sound like you. You peaked so early and with hardly any of the growing pains most people in your profession go through. How do you do better than that? How do you top yourself? Because, of course, people expect you to."

"There you go. It stinks. It more than stinks. It's the worst."

"Yeah. Now that you put it that way ..." She laughs, which is a surprise, given the nature of the topic. "Leave it to you to make me look at her in a different way. Isn't it usually the other way around? Aren't I the one telling you how silly you're acting?"

"Would you use the word *silly*? I'd use the word ... *charming*."

"I would not." She snorts. But at least she's not being all down on her sister anymore.

And she's not asking pointed questions about the time I spent alone with Kellen.

I wasn't kidding when I told her I don't remember what we talked about. Nothing specific. I do remember he told me about his family, his job, his apartment. Basic cocktail-party small talk. He asked about my family. I told him about my parents. Grandmother and Peter. I do remember that.

I also remember that he thought it was pretty neat, the two of them getting together after so many years. And I remember thinking then that I thought he was pretty neat for feeling that way.

I still do.

I think he's pretty neat in general. A little temperamental maybe. Grumpy at times. But a decent soul.

He didn't have to stay with me on the bus. He didn't have to be nice about it when he did either.

"Tomorrow morning is snorkeling," Hayley reminds me, blowing a sigh through pursed lips.

"I think that sounds like fun!"

"So, you're gonna do it?"

"Probably not."

"Kitty."

"Don't try to strong-arm me into it either. I need to work down here too."

"You are not going to do any such thing," she growls. "You deserve the time off. And if you don't come snorkeling—which will disappoint me, I'm not gonna lie—you'd better do something fun instead. Which means not working."

"I have to at least take notes if I hope to remember anything I see down here. And I have to monitor my social media feed. I've been posting pics but not responding to any comments." I raise my pitch, mimicking Maggie. *"Interaction, sweetie. It's all about interaction."*

"You do her voice way too well."

"If she'd stop saying things worth mimicking, I wouldn't have a reason to practice."

"Who do you practice it with? You live alone. Do you randomly talk to yourself in Maggie's voice?"

I turn to the water, raising a magazine in front of my face. "Shush."

"Because I think that's how Norman Bates got his start."

"Quiet, pest."

"Hey, girls!"

That gets our attention. We both look to the left, where Kylie and the rest of her bridesmaids have set up shop. Their chairs are in a circle, their feet in the center.

There's a whole lot of tanned skin and acrylic nails in that circle.

"Hey," Hayley calls back in a halfhearted sort of way. Like, *I have to talk to you because you started it, but I wouldn't have if you hadn't said anything.*

"You should come over here and hang out with us!" one of them calls out.

I recognize her as one of the girls who was flirting with Brandon on the bus.

The second girl adds, "Don't worry! The elevation over here is the same as over there! Just in case you're afraid of heights!"

"Oh, hell no." Hayley scrambles out of her chair while Kylie clearly chides the girls for being mean.

While all I can do is sit in my chair, wondering what the heck I did to insult them.

Then, I break out of my stupor in time to reach for her. "You don't have to do this. Don't start trouble." Though I know, even as I'm saying it, that she didn't start anything.

"Do me a favor, okay?" Hayley stands with her back to me, hands on her hips. "Keep your nasty little opinions to yourself. And keep your hands off my brother."

"Okay," I whisper, eyes darting back and forth between her and the circle of girls.

But it's not okay.

"You wanna know why we're not over there with you? Because you're ridiculous and vapid, and the only reason I'm on the same island with any of you is because I have to be for my sister. That's it. So, pretend we're not here together. Got it? Thanks in advance."

She then plops down in her chair and orders another drink without so much as a glance in their direction.

I don't know if I'm scared of her or if I want to kiss her.

"Sorry," she mumbles, staring straight ahead. "I couldn't keep quiet. Nobody messes with you or Brandon. End of story."

"I agree. On the Brandon thing anyway. I would never want you to get in a fight because of me."

"It's no big deal. Trust me. I would've said something about Brandon sooner rather than later anyway. You should've seen them hanging over him. He's too good for this world."

"So are you." I can't help but giggle, though I'm still mortified. "You know you're never going to like anybody your brother dates until you start looking at him as a man and not, like, some unworldly man-child."

"Probably not. You're right."

Kylie comes at us like a storm. A very blonde, very angry storm. "What the hell was that supposed to be?" she hisses, arms crossed over her midsection.

"It was supposed to be me telling your so-called friends they're a bunch of mean girls who need to grow up and get a life." She looks up at her sister, shrugging. "I mean, you were there. You didn't see it? You didn't hear it?"

"You're the one who needs to grow up." Kylie casts a look over her shoulder. "You could've just come over. They were trying to be friendly."

"They were being nasty, catty bitches, and we both know it. I have no time for that. Just because you do doesn't mean I have to put up with it. So, get that idea out of your head right now, okay?"

"It's my wedding, Hayley."

"No kidding, Kylie. And until now, I was fine with playing nice, pretending to be friends. But not when my best friend is being insulted for having a panic attack over something completely normal. I'm sorry, but if you bothered to know me at all, you wouldn't expect me to put up with it for a second."

Meanwhile, here I am, sinking deeper into my chair.

I'm the reason they're having this fight—somewhat. How am I not supposed to feel like I did something wrong?

It looks like the rest of this week is going to be even more uncomfortable than I imagined.

Chapter Nine

ONE THING IS clear by the time I reach the dock, where we're scheduled to gather for the snorkeling session.

Absolutely no one is in any condition to go snorkeling.

Well, not no one. There is one person in particular who is over-the-moon excited to get started.

At least, she's doing her best to convince us she is.

"I've always wanted to do this!" Kylie is in a one-piece suit, its white color standing out against her tanned skin, and she looks absolutely radiant.

Though, on closer inspection, the lines etched over the bridge of her nose, between her knitted brows, tell a different story. The girl is wound tight enough to pop. No matter how hard she smiles, it's obvious she's a mess inside.

There is only a handful of us out here. Hayley is on her way down, I know. She had a surprise phone call from the office that needed her attention. I want to tell Kylie about this, to explain why her sister isn't with us yet.

Silly me, thinking that would be the biggest problem this morning.

Somebody needs to tell Zack's groomsmen to lay off with the heavy drinking. Just like yesterday morning, they all look like death warmed over. Even worse since this is the second hangover in a row.

For all I know, it's much more than the second. Maybe this is the sort of thing they do every night in their real lives, though if it is, I have to wonder how they manage to hold down jobs. I know that if I were their boss and they showed up every morning with a green color to their skin and the vague look of being on the verge of throwing up, they wouldn't work for me for very long.

Call me crazy.

"I might sit this one out." That's Mitch, one of the groomsmen. He's speaking low, like anything louder will make his head fall off. "I, um, don't feel so good."

"Is there anywhere to sit down?" asks Dave, another of Zack's friends.

Our instructor looks to Kylie, his brow lifting. "Maybe this isn't the best time for your group to do this?"

I barely manage to keep from cringing openly since I can only imagine how she'll take this.

Her jaw twitches, and her eyes narrow, but she maintains that overly bright tone of voice. "Maybe we don't all have to do it, but I did book this time."

I can tell what she's not saying out loud since it would be rude.

She paid for this time. And now, the buffoons her fiancé is friends with are ruining it.

All except for one.

While even Zack looks a little green around the gills, Kellen is as fresh as a daisy. It's like he's living in some parallel universe, outside the rest of them. I know I saw all of them together at the bar just off the lobby last night. He was with them.

Maybe he's only drinking soft drinks? Maybe he knows his limits?

"I'm game," he announces. "I've always wanted to do this too."

Kylie shoots him a grateful look.

The instructor shrugs. "Okay, let me demonstrate how to use the equipment."

Which is precisely the moment when Mitch throws up all over the place.

And I do mean, all over. I'm glad I'm standing nowhere near him since the splash radius is pretty extensive.

Everybody jumps back in horror. Dave covers his mouth with his hand and ducks behind a tree where he, too, throws his guts up. The smell is appalling. I turn away with my hand over my mouth and nose, gagging a little.

"Everybody, back away," the instructor barks.

I can tell he's disgusted, both from the smell and from the fact that these people can't get their act together.

And he's hardly the only one.

I shoot a look Kylie's way, only to find her practically simmering, glowing bright red on the verge of turning purple.

"Are you kidding me?" she demands, and there's not so much as a hint of the sweet, smiling girl who was just with us a few moments ago. "Are you determined to ruin this? What the hell is wrong with you?"

Obviously, it's a rhetorical question, but even if it wasn't, there wouldn't be time to offer an answer because she turns on her heel and runs away.

My heart sinks. The rest of her bridesmaids are too busy holding their noses and reacting in disgust to think about following her. It seems like I'm the only one with the nerve to do it.

Or the only one with a death wish since there's no way to predict how she'll react. Granted, I'm not the one who puked all over the place, but there's a reason the expression don't shoot the messenger exists.

She's too quick for me, and I quickly lose sight of her when she rounds a bend in the path. It forks off in two directions. One direction heads for the main building, and the other goes toward one of the pools.

I decide to go toward the pool since I doubt she would want to run to the lobby in tears. She wants to be alone.

And, no, the fact that I'm determined to find her when she wants to be alone is not lost on me. But the poor girl needs somebody to talk to, somebody to sympathize. And if there's one thing I have for her right now, it's sympathy.

I follow the path then, which brings me to the open, semicircular bar situated several feet from what's referred to as the quiet pool. In other words, it's the pool where people are expected to behave themselves. The bar is empty at this time of the morning, but a certain bright white swimsuit catches my eye.

She's crying. Holding her face in her hands, shoulders shaking. It's the sort of moment I feel bad about stepping into, but the thought of her crying alone now of all times just about breaks my heart.

"Hey, Kylie." I touch her shoulder with a tentative hand.

We've never been close or anything. We know each other and have been to a few of the same events, thanks to our connection to Hayley, but there's hardly what you'd call intimate friendship between us.

She jumps a little at this, her head whipping around. Her eyes are watery, her nose red. "Oh. Hey, Kitty. Sorry. I didn't think anybody was out here."

"You don't have to apologize." I go through my tote for tissues, which I hand to her. "Here you go. What can I do for you? What do you need?"

A soft laugh bursts from her when she's finished blowing her nose. "You're a really nice person. I've always thought that."

"Thank you." Random but appreciated.

"You're probably the only person who'd find me here and ask what I needed. That's what I mean." She sighs, combing her mussed hair with her fingers. "Mom would remind me how happy I'm supposed to be right now, basically shaming me for having feelings. Dad would threaten to kill whoever made me cry. Zack would smother me. Any of my girlfriends would … I don't even know. Probably bring me a drink and scream, *Yaaaaassss*, in my face until I knew I'd better stop crying or they'd never let up."

I have to laugh at that because I can totally see it happening. It's exactly the sort of thing her girls would do.

Well, not all of them. One in particular would sooner rip out her own tongue.

"Hayley would ask why you're crying and what you need," I murmur.

She stops short of rolling her eyes. Barely. "My sister? She can't stand me. We're oil and water."

"I wouldn't take it that far. I'll grant you the *oil and water* thing, but it's not because you're different. It's because you're so similar."

There's an empty chair next to her, and I drop into it. "It doesn't help that your parents always compare the three of you, and she always comes in last place. I know it hurts her. She works really hard and is pretty spectacular in her own right."

"I agree. I do, Kitty," she insists, making an X over her heart with one finger. "I think she's amazing. So does Brandon. I don't see why Mom and Dad always act like there's a competition among us. Maybe they think it fuels us to do better. I don't know."

"It's not fair."

"No, it really isn't. I should've said something to her a long time ago." She looks at me, eyes still red-rimmed and watery. "Thanks for putting it to me that way. I needed to hear it."

"No problem."

"And I have to tell you something." She turns to me, facing me head-on. "I am so sorry for what the girls said to you the other day. That whole thing about the panic attack you had. I felt really bad about it, but I was more upset over Hayley starting trouble. I know she doesn't like the girls. I want everybody to get along."

Her chin trembles. "Why isn't this going the way I had it in my head?"

"Nothing ever does," I whisper, taking her hand. "And that sucks, and I'm sorry. I can't tell you how many things I've planned out in my head, down to the last detail—I mean, beginning to end, leaving nothing out. Do you know how much of it goes exactly the way I wanted?"

"But I've worked so hard."

"And anybody with eyes can see that. Ever since I got here, I've been marveling over all the work you've done. The baskets? Girl."

She offers a slight smile. "I wanted everybody to feel welcome and appreciated."

"It was a great touch." Maybe a little much, but … "Everything you've done is perfect. Exquisite. But I have to tell you something, and I hope you don't take it the wrong way."

She braces herself.

"It's not the end of the world, believe me. I think you should relax now. Let go. You're holding on so tight, like your fist is always this way." I hold up a fist, clenched as tight as I can until it shakes. "See? This is you holding on to what everything is supposed to be like. Managing every second of the day. It hurts. It's no fun."

I open my fist, cupping my hand. "This is how you could be. Accepting what happens. Holding it but letting it go when something else comes along for you to enjoy and remember. You're not enjoying this. You'll only remember being stressed. That isn't fair. I'm afraid it'll only make you sad when you look back."

Her face scrunches up, like she's thinking hard about this.

"My God, you're right," she eventually states. Her shoulders slump. "Damn it. I'm missing out on my wedding. I've put months of work into planning this, and I won't have anything to remember but being annoyed when we fall behind schedule or getting mad at Hayley for fighting with the girls."

"Yeah, that's probably true." I'm trying my best to be gentle with her since I'm sure this can't be easy to hear. "But, hey, there's plenty of time for you to still be present in the moment. We're only on day three. You can relax and let go and make the most of what's left."

"I have to admit, I don't know if I'll be able to do it. That's not my style." She snickers, casting a rueful look my way. "Big surprise, I'm sure."

"No comment," I whisper, and she laughs. Thank goodness.

"I can try though. I want to have fun."

"You can do it. Tell Zack how you feel. He can talk you off the ledge whenever it seems like things are slipping out of your control and you get that tight feeling in your chest. Tell Hayley too." She rolls her eyes. "I mean it," I add.

"You know she won't listen."

"I think she will. I know she loves you, but you two would get along better, I think, if she saw you as a human being instead of this perfect person you give the impression of being. Like you never make a mistake or have things you regret. If she could relate to you, she'd get along with you. I swear. I've been putting up with her for years."

It's nice to hear her laugh after so many days of wondering whether her teeth would break if she clenched them any tighter.

She surprises me with a fierce hug. "Thanks. I'm so glad Hayley has a friend like you."

"Do me a favor and tell her that, okay?"

She giggles and nods. "While I'm at it, I'll ask Zack to ask his guys to lay off the booze. They're treating this week like they're back on spring break or something."

"I know, right? It's completely irresponsible, and you couldn't have imagined that. But maybe, you know … maybe only the people who feel up to it have to go on the excursions and activities. Hayley's probably down at the dock right now. Her boss called just as we were leaving the room. I know she wanted to snorkel, and so did Brandon."

"Yes, I guess I can't expect so much from certain people." She hugs me again. "Thanks. I think I'd better go and apologize to the instructor."

"Heck no. Let them do it. They're the ones who made fools of themselves. You take care of you and your fiancé."

She seems to like this idea. Her eyes even brighten a little before she hurries away in the direction of the snorkelers.

Maybe this morning isn't a total waste. If I helped take the stick out of her butt, or however Hayley likes to put it, that's fine with me.

The sound of a throat being cleared makes me gasp and spin in my chair.

"Sorry." Kellen holds up both hands, freezing in place on the other side of the semicircular bar. "I didn't mean to scare you."

I laugh, nervous. "You have a habit of being nearby when I least expect you."

"Yeah, I'm stealthy." He looks away from me, to where Kylie is still visible on her way to the group. "No, really, I was looking for her. Zack was worried about her. He didn't know what to do. If he ran off after her, it would make things look worse than they were and bring the mood down even further. So, I offered."

"Best-man duties."

"Something like that." He eyes me with a grin. "You were too fast for me."

"Sorry. I didn't mean to step on your toes."

"No, no, believe me, I'm glad you did. If I had caught up with her first, I don't know what I would've said. It probably would've come off sounding stupid. You knew exactly how to handle the situation."

Modesty compels me to shrug this off, though I can't help but warm a little inside at the sound of his approving tone. Like he's impressed.

"I've been paying attention to her. Trying to figure her out. Hayley granted me a little extra insight yesterday too." I glance his way with a smile. "But, hey, don't sell yourself short. You knew just what to say to me when I was freaking out inside the bus. A lot of people might've ignored me or handed me over to Hayley since she knows me so well. You didn't. You kept me calm."

He scoffs and tries to brush it off. "Yeah, well, Hayley already had her hands full with trying to keep her brother safe from the big, bad blondes."

"Still, you didn't have to. So, I think you might've been able to get through to Kylie."

When he reaches me, he kisses my cheek. "You're a real person. Decent. Substantial. Worth knowing."

My cheeks flush. "I have to admit, I've never heard those words used to describe me before."

"Then, you aren't talking to the right people." He squeezes my shoulder gently but firmly. "Just think, if you hadn't talked sense into her, Kylie could've ended up regretting this entire week. You did something special today because you're special."

I'm so overwhelmed; I don't know what to say. I guess anything would sound empty and silly at this point—not to mention the fact that my tongue is completely tied, useless. I can only glow in the warmth of his approval.

"Be careful," I warn him. "I might start getting a big head if you don't take it easy." Because, obviously, I'm the queen of deflection when there's nothing else I can think to say.

"Fine, be that way." He backs away with a wide smile, holding his hands up like he did before. "Keep pretending you don't know how cool you are. I'll get through to you before the week is over."

As he wanders off, all I can do is hope he keeps trying.

Chapter Ten

"YOU DON'T HAVE to do this if you don't want to."

Missy shook her head, determined. "No, I'm going to. So long as it means shutting their mouths."

She threw a look over her shoulder, where the mean-girl bridesmaids looked on. There was nothing in the world so obvious as somebody trying to pretend they weren't paying attention when they clearly were.

Followed only by how obvious they made it that they couldn't stand her.

"Them?" Trent snickered, shaking his head. "What the hell does it matter what they think? Or even what they say? Nobody with a brain in their head would pay attention anyway."

She looked him up and down, not even bothering to make it seem like she wasn't studying him. "You're just saying that."

"No, I'm not just saying it. I mean it. They're jokes, all of them. Don't you know that?"

"I know it. I just didn't think you did."

He had a nice laugh, the sort that made a person want to laugh with him. The sort of laugh that lightened a person's spirits.

A miraculous laugh, since not much else in the world could've inspired Missy to giggle while standing on a cliff, overlooking the crystal-clear water below.

How was she to know she was afraid of heights? She had been all over the world, had gone to the top of the Eiffel Tower, had taken a hot air balloon ride. She had certainly enjoyed the view from more than one Manhattan penthouse.

There was a difference in all those situations when compared to the one she was in now.

A guard rail had been involved. Or a window. Something to hold on to, something between her and the free fall.

Not so much now. Standing at the edge of a cliff, looking down, down, down to the rocks below. Water battered those rocks, and how could she not picture her body being battered too?

Her broken, bruised, bloodied body. After falling and hitting approximately every rocky ledge on the way down.

"I guess now isn't the time to tell you how clumsy I am."

"Maybe you shouldn't think about it," Trent suggested.

"It's just that I tend to trip over thin air. If there's any way for me to hurt myself, I'll find it."

"Terrific. I'll make it a point to stay far away from you."

Her head snapped around, and she could just feel her eyes bulging as she glared at Trent and his smirking face. "Thanks a lot!"

"Hey, what am I supposed to do? Stand here and wait for you to fall against me, knocking us both over the edge?"

It was only then that she figured out he was kidding around. When she cracked a smile, he smiled too.

"See? It's not so dire. Don't think about what you don't want to happen because that's a surefire way to get what you don't want."

He looked away from her, over the water stretching out in all directions. "Just look at how beautiful it is. Stand absolutely still, take a deep breath, and think about how lucky we are to be here. Right here, right in this moment. Today. When the water is so clear and the breeze is so warm. Can you smell the firepits back at the resort, where they're getting ready to start roasting the pigs for tonight's party?"

"I guess now isn't the time to tell you that I'm a vegetarian."

He laughed again. "You're tough. Tell me you smell the wood burning."

"I do. It makes me think of camping when I was little. I used to go to the campgrounds with my parents and grandparents every summer. They had a trailer there big enough for the five of us."

"I can tell just by the way your voice changed that those are happy memories."

"The best. I used to look forward to it all year long. And then, when it finally came around, time slipped past. I wanted so much to hold on to it, but it was like blinking my eyes, and poof! It was over."

"That's how it is. Life, I mean."

From the corner of her eye, Missy watched as he slid his hands into his pockets. His shoulders rose and fell as he took a deep breath—broad shoulders, thick, just like his thick arms and thighs, which she only now realized she'd been paying attention to.

"When we try to hold on too tight, that's when we lose what we're holding on to. We can only enjoy things when we let go."

If this had happened under any other circumstances, she would've rolled her eyes. If one of her friends had told her of an experience like this, where a handsome stranger gave excellent life advice while standing on a cliff, she would've told them to get a grip.

Yet here she was, and there he was. And in that moment, he was the only thing keeping her from launching into a full-fledged panic attack that would have probably sent her over the edge. Literally.

Okay, so maybe I changed the details of the situation a little bit. A lot actually. At least my heroine had the courage to get off the bus. I couldn't even manage that.

And, sure, I might or might not have shared my own wisdom through my hero. Sue me. What I said has already had an almost-magical effect on Kylie, who, since yesterday morning, has loosened up to the point where everybody has mentioned it.

At least, according to Hayley, who still can't get over the difference.

"You know, she actually said it was up to us whether

or not we wanted to go parasailing. Did the aliens come and replace her when I wasn't looking?"

I only smiled and shrugged. "Maybe she finally figured out this is supposed to be fun and memorable. That looks different to different people. To some, fun means parasailing and snorkeling. To others, it means getting drunk off their butt every night."

"That's another thing! I went down to the bar last night, figuring the guys would be there and they weren't!"

I only offered another Mona Lisa smile.

I've never been one to brag after all. Besides, if Kylie hasn't mentioned anything about our conversation, I won't either.

Hayley decided to go parasailing, but I begged off. I really do need to finish taking notes on this new project.

And judging by the fact that I already have a few chapters at least roughly sketched out, my creative muse was just dying to get out and have a little fun.

It must be the fresh air and all the sunshine. Much more sunshine than I ever get back home, cooped up in my apartment.

Yet the thought of my apartment makes my heart clench a little. I can't be homesick, can I? It hasn't even been a week. People take vacations all the time. I've even been known to go away now and then, shockingly enough.

Still, as divine as it is to sit on my patio with the

beach just inches from my feet and nothing but the blue sky above me, I sort of miss my routine. Morning yoga in front of the window, letting the sunshine stream in. Ordering from my favorite Chinese place for lunch. With or without Matt.

I'm still not totally cool with him, even after almost a week. In fact, I would rather not think about him right now.

Still, he's part of my routine. So is Phoebe. And I miss her even if I don't miss her owner very much and would like to drown him a little if he were here with me.

Maybe I'm getting too set in my ways. I need to mix things up. That's never a good thing, falling into a rut.

And if the amount of work I've already gotten done in only a couple of hours is any indication, a change in routine is good for my creativity.

It also helps that I have solid source material to work with.

In other words, the fact that Kellen has been so sweet. Much sweeter than I would've originally imagined. Of course, I'm working that into my outline too. My hero doesn't start off all sweetness and sunshine. In fact, I don't want him to ever be that way.

After all, a little bit of salt brings out the flavor of the dish. You can't have all sweetness, all the time.

And I think, after these last several days of getting to know him, finding Kellen's got salt and sweet in equal measure makes him more interesting. More intriguing. It makes those sweet moments all the sweeter and more worthwhile.

I never would've imagined that coming here for a week would open my eyes this way.

Maybe I should get my publisher to reimburse Hayley and Kylie for the costs.

Cracking my knuckles, I get back to work.

"Hey, Missy! You should try looking over the edge!"

Missy shot a look in the direction of the group of bridesmaids, where two of them were chortling like what they'd just heard was the funniest thing that had ever happened. She had never been very good at defending herself. It was easier to stand back, to be passive, to let things happen without too much fuss.

In other words, she'd spent her entire life trying to avoid confrontation.

Yet, for some reason, things looked different now.

Maybe it was the sea air, fresh and salty. The scent of the firepits carrying her way on the breeze.

Maybe it was the fact that she had managed to stand here, in this spot, and not drop dead of fright—or go over the edge, screaming the whole way down.

It could be the presence of the man standing next to her, someone who didn't say a word but whose jaw had visibly tightened at the sound of giggles at Missy's expense.

Whatever it was, it heated her blood and stiffened her spine.

"I sure wouldn't want to land in the water without a flotation device to hang on to. Maybe you could help me out, Lexi?" With that, Missy shot a very pointed look at the girl's way overinflated chest.

Lexi's face went red, her eyes narrowing until they were barely slits. "I guess some of us would sink pretty quickly, wouldn't we?" She stared at Missy's butt, snickering.

But Missy had come to love her curves, and she never would have body-shamed anybody who wasn't being a wretched, nasty witch. Sometimes though, people needed to be put in their place.

Which was why she took a chance, winding her arm around Trent's and smiling up at him. "You wouldn't let me sink, would you?" she asked.

His flash of a smile told her he understood. "No way. If you went over, I would go after you."

"My hero," she cooed, squeezing his arm a little for effect.

The widening of his smile told her he understood—that he might have even encouraged it a little.

Still, she had to be sure. On their way back to the bus, she whispered, "Sorry if I laid it on a little too thick back there."

"Are you kidding?" His eyes met hers, and for the first time, something danced in them. Something she hadn't seen before. A new light. "If that had gone on much longer, I might've had to kiss you in front of everybody just to shut their mouths."

Her insides fluttered at the thought.

And she wondered if it was crazy to wish Lexi hadn't

given up so easily.

Chapter Eleven

"WOW." THAT'S PRETTY much all I can say after stepping into the banquet room, where the rehearsal dinner is set to take place.

Actually, that's not quite true. I haven't fully entered the room yet, instead lingering in the doorway. It's like I've completely forgotten how to walk.

Mostly because I'm overwhelmed by how beautiful everything is. If I didn't know better, I would think this was the reception rather than the rehearsal dinner. Lush floral arrangements as centerpieces, candlelight flickering in every corner and on every table.

It was a beautiful rehearsal too. Picture-perfect. I snapped a few shots with my phone and plan to show them to Kylie. If she wants, I'll send them to her since they are truly spectacular.

Not that my photography skills had anything to do with it. It just so happened that she and Zack were standing on a bluff overlooking the water, and the sun was on its way down beneath the horizon as they held hands and looked into each other's eyes.

Really, I couldn't have come up with a better image if I tried.

If things go even half as well tomorrow, this wedding will be one for the history books.

Now, there is the matter of a serious party about to go down. I hope, for the sake of everybody involved with the wedding party, that it wraps up early and doesn't involve too much alcohol, though I see bridesmaids and groomsmen already approaching the bar.

On the opposite side of the room, there's an extensive buffet. All sorts of seafood along with a carving station, where I heard prime rib will be served. Salads, pastas, a huge cheeseboard. And I do love cheese.

Naturally, me being me, my attention drifts to the dessert table. I'm going to have to become acquainted with several of the offerings there. Good thing they're all small servings.

"Well, this is stunning." Hayley looks around with a smile, and I'm glad to see it. Instead of coming up with a snarky comment about how her sister always has to go above and beyond, she seems downright pleased to see how nicely everything has come together.

"Did you expect anything less?"

"No, now that you mention it."

We make our way to the bar and manage to chat up the few members of the wedding party who are willing and able to speak to both of us. Meaning the guys basically since the girls are still carrying a chip on their shoulder after that little confrontation with Hayley on the beach.

Some people just can't let things go. Honestly, I'm the one they were making fun of, but they're the ones sulking.

"I'm amazed Briggs isn't here. I thought the two of them were joined at the hip."

I heard that. Sarah. She meant for me to hear it. I recognize her as the one who made the comment about my little freak-out on the mountain.

How funny.

I mean, I wrote a situation so similar to this. Where the bridesmaids were jealous of my heroine because the best man paid close attention to her.

Yet not until just now did it occur to me that the same thing might be happening in real life. Maybe I picked it up subconsciously, and it's finally bubbling its way to the surface.

I never considered myself slow on the uptake before. Clearly, I have a few things to learn about myself.

She only wants to get a rise out of me. I realize this, which is why I don't say anything.

Though I'm not going to pretend I didn't hear it.

I happen to be the granddaughter of one of Manhattan's most respected and, let's be honest, most feared personalities. It's not only Grandmother's blue eyes that I inherited.

It's her icy stare. A stare which I'm all too happy

to demonstrate.

"Oh my God, it's like your grandmother is here with us," Hayley whispers, which would make me laugh under any other circumstance. I mean, how perfect is that? It's like she's reading my mind.

But the stare isn't quite as effective if I'm smiling, so I don't react. I don't so much as blink.

Sarah snickers but turns away. I've won this round.

"I think you deserve a drink." Hayley orders for me since she obviously knows what I prefer after spending so many happy hours together.

I settle for leaning against the bar, feeling pretty darn powerful, so long as I'm being honest.

No wonder Grandmother stares icily so much of the time. A girl could get addicted to that sort of power.

As I survey my domain with all the pride of a lioness, one tiny thought tickles the back of my mind.

Where is Kellen?

Darn it. I told myself I wasn't going to let this happen. That I wouldn't spend my time looking for him, searching the room for him. That I wouldn't get caught up in where he was, what he was thinking and doing.

Yet here I am. Such a sucker.

"I'm sure he'll be here soon." Hayley flashes a sly smile as she hands me my drink.

"Who?"

"Oh, come on!" She doesn't bother to be polite and hide her laughter.

I choose to sip my drink since arguing will only leave me wanting to slap her silly in front of all these people.

After all, she does have to look nice for the wedding tomorrow. Kylie might have loosened up about a lot of things, but I doubt she would appreciate a bridesmaid with a handprint on her cheek.

It's like she heard me thinking about her. Kylie walks in with Zack's arm around her waist, laughing about something he must've said just before they entered the room. And it's a genuine laugh, not the forced kind from a few days ago. She's like a new person.

Though that doesn't stop her from being a little critical about the placement of a few chafing dishes along the buffet.

Hayley notices too. "We can't have everything." She smirks with a shake of her head.

"Kitty!" Hayley's mother spots me and hurries over, holding her arms out. "I've been meaning to catch you."

"Oh look, something else that I absolutely have to handle right this very minute." Hayley scurries away before her mom reaches us.

I barely manage not to roll my eyes.

I wish Kellen were here to see this. It's exactly the sort of exit I tried describing to him when we first met.

The family matriarch possesses the blonde good looks that were passed to her children. Her husband is tall and dark while she's the blue-eyed Nordic beauty. I can imagine Hayley looking like her thirty years from now.

Lucky girl.

Her smile is warm, wide as she takes me by the hands. "I just wanted to say how nice it is to have you with us. Hayley is always talking about how hard you work, and it's great to see you relaxing and enjoying yourself. You are enjoying yourself, aren't you?"

I'd have to be a straight-up idiot not to be enjoying myself, but that's hardly the sort of thing I can say to somebody's mom. "Absolutely. This is all incredible. I did need a break."

She gets a very motherly look on her face, wagging a finger and everything. "I've heard you've been working though."

"Well, between you and me, there's so much inspiration here."

When Kellen appears in the doorway, it's like my eyes immediately follow his movement. He's basically a magnet I can't help but be drawn to.

And the man can rock a linen suit like nobody's business. That helps.

Hayley's mom chuckles softly. "Yes. Plenty of inspiration, I see." Her laughter floats away with her as she continues around the room, performing her mother-of-the-bride duties.

So, what? Has everybody been talking about Kellen and me? I'm starting to feel conspicuous.

Especially since he finds me right away. I mean, I am standing near the bar. That could be why he makes his way over here so quickly.

Though that doesn't account for the way he zeroes in on me while waiting his turn. "You look very nice," he murmurs.

"Hayley forced me into this dress," I confess.

It's strapless and a little shorter than I would normally wear to a family-related function. Light and breezy, too, so a gust of wind might send it up over my face.

If it was long enough to reach my face anyway.

"I think she made the right move. It looks great on you. Then again, what do I know? I'm just a guy. You know we don't know much about these things."

The way he is looking at me tells a totally different story, the sort of story that makes me feel warm and fluttery all over. One thing this dress is no good at is hiding the goose bumps suddenly covering my arms and legs.

"Hey, Briggs." Sarah and one of her friends whose name I can't remember—the other one who was pestering Brandon on the bus—approach him from both sides. "You'll save a dance for us tomorrow, right?"

It takes effort to keep my expression neutral, I'll admit, but I think I do a pretty good job of it. I don't believe any innocent passerby would know just how much I would love to claw this girl's eyes from her face, for instance.

"I don't know." He shrugs, chuckling. "I'm not such a great dancer."

"Oh, come on!" She flutters her eyelashes and grabs his arm. "I remember that night in the city. When we all met up at the club. Did you forget all about it already? It wasn't even two months ago."

Yes, she needs to be clawed. Like, severely.

Kellen's gaze darts over to me for the briefest second, not even the length of a heartbeat, before he looks at her again. "Honestly, I did forget all about that. I think I was pretty wasted that night. I promised Zack I would take it easy this week, for his sake, in case he needs anything." He pats her hand and loosens his arm from her grip before stepping up to place his drink order.

Leaving Sarah and me face-to-face.

As usual, I included a little bit of myself in my current heroine. Not only the fact that she didn't know she was afraid of heights until she was smack dab in the middle of a situation involving them, but also the way she preferred to avoid confrontation.

I might try to avoid it, but I will stick up for myself if I have to. I just always hope I don't. So, it's unusual for my blood to boil when I see the nasty, judgmental look on her face.

It's even more unusual for me to shrug, lifting an eyebrow, looking her up and down. Silently reminding her how forgettable she is. Not to mention, how completely transparent. She struts off in a huff and I let my body relax.

I don't know what Kellen was up to before we met, aside from the situation with the girl who stood him up, and I don't care very much.

Though if he really did hook up with this girl, I'd have to wonder about his taste in women.

"Sorry about that," he whispers once we're alone again—as alone as we can be in the middle of a party anyway. "She lays it on a little thick, doesn't she?"

I lift my glass to my lips, shrugging. "Does she? I didn't notice."

He laughs. "Right. You didn't notice. Cute."

Then, he glances her way, sighing. "That was a mistake. I know I don't owe any explanations. Honestly, there aren't any. Just one of those things. Regrettable. Drunken."

"At least now, I know I didn't do anything to earn her attitude."

I shouldn't have said that.

His expression shifts to one of surprise. "She's giving you attitude?"

"Don't worry about it."

"No, tell me. Who in their right mind—"

I cut that off with a wave of my hand. "Listen, I'm no angel. Don't mistake me for one. There are people in the world who don't like me. I'm not a little Goody Two–shoes."

"I never said you were, but you're not one of these backbiting, catty bitches either." When I wince, he winces too. "Sorry. I guess I feel a little too comfortable around you."

"I've never had anybody apologize to me for that before." I make it a point to smile, so he'll smile too.

"Hors d'oeuvres?" A server pops up at my elbow, almost like magic. He's carrying a tray of stuffed mushrooms.

"Yes, thank you." The fact is, I'm starving, and I don't want to let the alcohol go to my head.

Though, honestly, it might be fun. Maybe it's time to drop the Goody Two–shoes persona and be slightly naughty. After all, it's clear more than a few people here think the two of us have something going on.

Maybe I should give them something to talk about, like the old song says.

And that's exactly what's going through my head as I pop the mushroom into my mouth and chew it a few times.

Before instantly regretting it.

I shove my way through the crowd in front of the bar, not bothering to excuse myself, and grab for the nearest napkin before spitting out what's left in my mouth.

"Too hot?" Kellen asks.

I shake my head, and already, I can feel my skin starting to itch. "There's horseradish in them. I'm allergic to horseradish. Who puts horseradish in stuffed mushrooms?"

Because I steer clear of anything even hinting at containing horseradish, it's been a while since I've had a reaction. But I remember too well what happens once one gets started.

Suffice it to say, my night has just come to an end.

"YOU ABSOLUTELY DO not have to do this."

"Stop scratching."

"I can't help it." I have to clench my fists and leave them at my sides as Kellen walks me back to my room after my hasty exit from the rehearsal dinner.

"It was either I walk you back or Hayley. I didn't want her to miss anything tonight."

"What about you? You're supposed to be there with Zack."

He waves this off, using the hand not holding a box of allergy medicine, so helpfully provided by the front-desk staff. "It's not the same. Hayley is Kylie's sister. Her only sister. This is important for them, for the whole family. I can always swing back over there once I'm sure you're taken care of."

"I don't need you to take care of me though. I appreciate it, but I don't need it."

He looks me up and down as we come to a stop in front of my door. I can only imagine how horrific I must look, and frankly, I would rather avoid all mirrors once we're inside.

"With all due respect, are you sure about that?" He leaves it there rather than continuing, which is good because I'm really not in the mood to deal with witty banter right now.

He follows me into the room and pours a glass of water from the carafe on my nightstand, so I can wash down two of the allergy pills. I know from experience that they work fairly quickly, though I'll still be sort of itchy for the rest of the night.

"Oh my God!" I can hardly study myself in the mirror over the dresser. I look like somebody gave a toddler red finger paint and let them go crazy all over my skin. I'm practically covered in polka dots.

"It's not that bad."

I know he's trying to be nice and he doesn't deserve it, but I roll my eyes at him anyway. "It's absolutely terrible. I can't believe I let this happen!"

"Like you said, who puts horseradish in stuffed mushrooms? That's so strange."

"I love stuffed mushrooms too."

When he snorts, I turn away from the mirror to glare at him.

"Sorry, it's just that you sounded so sad. Like the stuffed mushrooms themselves had ruined your night."

I snicker a little when I look at it that way, and I can tell he's glad to see it. "Just my luck."

"It could've been worse, I guess. Like some sort of deadly allergy."

I notice he makes himself right at home, sitting

on the edge of the bed. It's a good thing I've been picking up after myself these last few days or else I might have been mortified even further at the thought of him seeing my unmentionables strewn all over the place.

But this is a resort—and a nice one. It's one thing to be a slob at home, but I wouldn't want the staff to think I was totally gross.

"That's true. Just a rash. As far as I know, it's the only thing I'm allergic to."

"Except for catty bi—women." He winks.

I have to grin in spite of the absolute hell my skin is putting me through. I just want to tear it off, and that's with the allergy pills making their way through my system.

His face scrunches. "You're really going through it right now, aren't you?"

"In a word, yes."

He pours more water and presses the glass into my hand. "You think a shower or bath might help? Maybe they've got something at the front desk or at the little store that has basic necessities, that you could use for this."

It warms my heart, how sweet he's acting.

But it would be selfish of me to indulge in this. "Seriously, you should go back to the party. I might call over to the store to see if they have something, but I doubt it. It's all right. I'll be fine in a couple of hours."

"Are you going to have dinner?"

"At some point, sure." Honestly, it's the last thing on my mind right now. I'm too busy trying to keep from scratching my skin off.

"What do you like?"

Is he for real?

"I don't know. I like seafood. Chicken. Tofu, though I don't think they have any of that here. Pasta. Most things really. The occasional burger."

He nods, firm. "Okay. Do me a favor and run yourself a bath. Anything that will help you feel a little better. Drink a ton of water. I'll be back in a half hour."

"What? Kellen, you don't have to—"

"A ton of water. Thirty minutes."

He's already out the door and halfway down the hall by the time I muster the energy to call his name again. It doesn't matter. He's a man on a mission.

What the heck have I gotten myself into this time?

There's one thing I'm not going to argue about. I need to drink lots of water to flush my system as quickly as possible. It's amazing really—the fact that just the tiniest bit of an allergen can set somebody off this way.

And to think, I spat most of the mushroom out. I can't imagine how much worse it would have been if I'd swallowed it.

At least the resort includes fancy bath products on the bathroom counters. There's a creamy bath foam among the bottles. I include a little of that in the water while running the bath, and then I slip out of my dress and hang it up on the hook on the back of the door.

So much for looking good tonight.

The bath is soothing though. Cool against my flushed skin. I soak for around fifteen minutes, until my fingers start to prune. By the time I'm rinsed off and wearing my pajamas, there's a knock at the door.

The man is standing there with a cart. He literally loaded a cart with trays and dishes and then wheeled it all the way over here.

"Kellen! What are you doing?"

"Making sure you have something to eat and something to help your skin feel better." I have no choice but to step aside as he starts pushing the cart into the room. "Don't think it was easy, getting this thing. The kitchen staff didn't want to give it up."

"I can't believe you went to this trouble!"

"It was no trouble." He takes a bowl from the cart's lower shelf and places it on my nightstand. "Plain oatmeal. To soothe your skin."

"Oh my gosh. You had them make oatmeal for me?"

"To be fair, I think they have it around all the time and just reheat it in the morning." He catches my eye and shrugs. "Even in the nicest resorts …"

I can't even pretend to be offended by this since just dabbing some on the back of one of my hands is like heaven. "I'm sure this is going to look pretty," I mutter in disgust with myself.

"Please. You could cover yourself in oatmeal from head to toe and be beautiful." He starts pulling lids from trays next. "We have prime rib, salmon, and a mix of scallops and shrimp in scampi sauce over capellini."

It all smells heavenly, but there are too many questions going through my head for me to enjoy it just yet. "Did you get this from the buffet?"

"They were pretty nice about it. I think, so long as we're being honest, they would be willing to do anything to avoid you freaking out over having a reaction."

"I wouldn't freak out." I mean, I would like to, but I know my limits.

"But they don't know that. I'm sure that in a place like this, they're used to guests flipping out over much less than what you're going through right now. Rich people tend to lose their cool at the drop of a hat." There's no humor in his voice now, which leads me to wonder just how well he knows what he's talking about.

"This is extraordinary. That probably sounds corny, but …" I spread my arms in a helpless shrug. There's nothing else to say.

It doesn't seem like I have to say anything else. He understands; I can tell he does.

"Sit down. Where would you like to eat? Do you want to go out to the patio? There's an actual table out there."

"I feel terrible about this. You should be having

a good time over in the banquet room."

He turns away from the cart, sliding his hands into his pockets with a sheepish sort of look on his face. "Can I be honest?"

"Sure …"

"There's only one person here tonight who I would want to talk to. No offense to either Kylie's or Zack's parents. No offense to Hayley or Brandon. But everybody else there bores the hell out of me. Maybe because we've all known each other for a long time. You're the only person who's caught my interest this week."

"So, I'm the novelty item catching your eye. Is that what you're telling me?"

A ghost of a smile flits across his face. "You're tough. Has anybody ever told you that?"

Now is not the time to be thinking about Matt, who would probably still be laughing at me for this whole allergic-reaction fiasco. "Yes, honestly."

"I wonder if you give them half as hard of a time as you're giving me right now. Come on. You have to eat something, and I'm hungry. This food smells too good to go to waste." Without another word, he wheels the cart out through the doors leading onto the patio.

I don't have any other choice but to follow him—and not just because I'm starving. It's the fact that having food in my system will help lessen the effects of the horseradish.

There's something about him. I can't put my

finger on it. He's strong-willed without being dominant. Maybe that's a sign of being completely comfortable in his skin. Yes, that's what it is. I don't think I've ever met anybody as comfortable with themself as he is.

I settle on the salmon, and he takes the prime rib. We decide to share the seafood pasta.

"Would you like some wine?" he asks.

"I wish I could have some, but I'm already afraid the drink I finished earlier isn't going to mix well with the allergy meds."

"Water it is." He plops a giant bottle in front of me while wearing a stern expression. "You'd better drink if you don't want to pass out before you get the chance to enjoy all this."

"Yes, sir." I take a healthy swig just to show him I'm serious. The fact is, I don't want to fall asleep. Not for as long as I can help it, not as long as he's here with me.

Besides, it wouldn't be fair for him to have gone to all this trouble, just to have me blink out on him halfway through the meal.

Not to mention the fact that the food is scrumptious.

"Oh my gosh." I have to close my eyes to savor the buttery salmon. "It tastes like it was caught today."

"I think they fly it in daily. At least, I wouldn't be surprised." Then, he groans after taking a bite of the prime rib. "Holy shit."

"I guess that means it's good?"

He cuts off a little bit and puts it on my plate. "Trust me, you will not regret it."

"No, but you might regret giving that to me," I groan after tasting it. *Holy mackerel, it's delicious.* "You might have to defend yourself against me. I get pretty serious about my food."

"Just when I thought I couldn't like you any more than I already do." He raises his glass of wine—there are two carafes underneath the cart, one of red and one of white since he clearly thought of everything—and I raise my water in response. "To eventful rehearsal dinners."

Indeed.

Though in spite of the itchy skin and the absolutely crushing embarrassment of having to leave the dinner early, I'm not sure I would have it any other way. Crazy as it sounds.

Chapter Thirteen

"WHOA. WHAT THE hell happened around here last night?"

The sound of Hayley's voice breaks through my deep sleep. I blink away the morning sunlight and then groan in mixed horror and disgust when I realize I slept all night with oatmeal on my face.

She's looking down at me with a wry grin. "What, did you have a beauty-regimen night? Did Briggs put oatmeal on his face too? Maybe a mud mask?"

"It's for the itching and swelling."

"I'm only teasing." She sits down next to me on the bed, wincing. "How are you feeling, sweetie?"

"Much better. Where the heck were you all night? Are you just getting in?"

She smiles, her chin dipping down. "I spent the night in Kylie's room. It was actually really fun."

"Really? That's so neat!"

"Besides, I figured …" She gives me a sly smile.

"You figured wrong. You have no idea what you're talking about if you think I was in any mood for any such thing last night."

"Again, teasing."

"Not to sound too needy, but how come you never even texted to ask if I was okay?"

She arches an eyebrow, reaching for the phone in her purse. "You think I never checked in? Trust me, I had a little talk with Briggs as he was loading the cart with food for you. He gave me his number, and I checked in with him all night."

Sure enough, there are at least a dozen messages from her to him, asking if I was doing okay. He kept her updated, letting her know I ate, that I was looking and feeling better. He told her we sat around, watching an old thriller on one of the movie channels, which we did after we finished eating.

But he was kind enough to leave out the part where I had oatmeal slathered all over my face the entire time. Not exactly my proudest or my most desirable moment.

"Thank you for checking up on me." I snicker. "Did anybody have anything to say about my sudden departure?"

The fact that she's so quick to get up from the bed and move across the room to her own bed tells me a lot.

"It's okay. I want to know. You would've been proud of me, staring that Sarah chick down the way I did."

"You did? How come you didn't tell me?"

"There really wasn't much time, was there? One

minute, everything was okay, and the next, I broke out in polka dots."

"Yeah, she tried to spread nastiness about you," Hayley admits. "Don't worry. Nobody takes her seriously. Even Kylie jumped to your defense, and honestly, it was pretty amazing to see."

That's enough to get me to sit up. "What did she say?"

"She told Sarah to mind her own business and to stop being mean toward somebody she likes. Kylie never stands up to any of those girls; I want you to understand that right off the bat. So, to hear her say that was just short of miraculous."

"Wow! I mean, I don't want to be the reason that they start fighting …"

"How many times do I have to tell you? You're not the reason. She is. For the most part, everybody was concerned about you. Briggs filled us all in and told us not to worry about it before he came back here."

She shakes her head, her eyebrows jumping up and down. "I don't know what you did to him, but you definitely had an effect. He was practically frenzied, Kitty. I'm not kidding. He wanted to make sure you had everything you needed, including that oatmeal."

"Speaking of which." I jump up out of bed to go to the bathroom and wash my face, which is no easy feat. I don't want to clog up the pipes with the oatmeal, so I have to try to take it off with a washcloth as carefully as I can before washing the rest away.

I should've known Hayley wouldn't be put off so easily. Just because I walked away from our conversation didn't mean she was going to let it go.

Watching from the doorway, she teases, "He likes you."

I catch her eye in the mirror. She's enjoying this way too much.

"What is this, middle school?"

"No. If it were middle school, I would sing, *Briggs and Kitty sitting in a tree …*"

"You're adorable, you know that?"

"Says the girl with dried-up oatmeal all over her face."

I stick my tongue out. "Okay, I like him too. Are you happy? You were right. He's a nice guy, we get along well, and who knows? Maybe I need some-body to look out for me a little bit since I clearly cannot take care of myself."

"You really haven't had very good luck this week, have you?"

"I think we both know it could be worse though."

"Knowing you? Without a doubt."

Now that my face looks a little more like my own and less like that of a horror-movie villain, I'm pleased with the results of my overnight oatmeal mask. The rest of my skin is back to normal too—thank goodness. I wouldn't want to show up in any pictures from the wedding, looking the way I did last night.

"So? Did he spend the night?"

I can't help but laugh at the very idea. "Once again, I was in no condition."

"I'm not saying anything had to happen. I was wondering if he slept over."

"No, he went back to his room. Honestly, I don't even remember that happening. I took a second dose of the meds, and that was enough to knock me out. I don't think I moved all night, to be honest."

"Aww, he tucked you in and left you to sleep. How cute."

"Would you shut up?"

"I'm not being snarky or sarcastic or anything. I really do think it's cute. Very sweet. I overheard Zack saying he's never seen Briggs act that way before over a girl, and they've known each other practically their whole lives."

Part of me sincerely wishes she would stop talking about things like this because all it does is make me like him more while convincing me of his feelings.

This is dangerous territory.

"I'm sure things won't be the same way once we go back to our regular lives."

"What makes you so sure?"

"Come on. It's fine to be flirty and sweet and cute while we're here, at the resort, and the rest of our lives are on the back burner. We'll both go back to work. He'll be out at the family's second home, probably reconnecting with old friends, and I'll be some girl he helped through a hard time during the wedding week."

"I don't think you give yourself nearly enough credit, but that's always been the case."

"You're biased."

"Listen, girl, I saw him last night. I saw the way he acted when you started getting all splotchy. He was really concerned. He didn't think twice about bringing you back to the room even though it meant leaving the party. He burst into the kitchen, demanding they provide oatmeal for you to soothe your skin since they were the ones who made you have a reaction."

My eyes widen in surprise.

"Yes, he did," she insists.

"Over me?"

"Over you, you dork. He really likes you. So, please, for the love of God, kiss the man tonight. At least do that much."

"Are you sure you don't want to be there to direct the whole thing?"

"You're impossible." She lets out an exasperated sigh before walking away. "Do what you need to do in there and make it snappy. I need to take a shower before the hair and makeup people get here."

Right. I'll be on my own for most of the day while she and her family and the other bridesmaids get ready.

That's fine by me, honestly, since I feel a little stiff and achy. My skin might look better, but I'm still slightly inflamed on the inside. I could use a little time with my project too.

I'm seated out on the patio with my laptop when Hayley sticks her head out.

"I'm headed over to the bridal suite now. I'll see you out there?"

"You sure will. Have fun, okay? Make sure to remind your sister to breathe and relax."

"You mean, the way you did?" She steps outside and throws her arms around my shoulders. "She told me last night. How you talked to her and made her feel better the day of the snorkeling lesson. I should've known you had something to do with it. It's like she's been a completely different person since then. And she's been a lot nicer to me too. She's been going out of her way to be, you know, sisterly. More so than she's ever been before."

"I didn't want to make it seem like everything was about me, so I didn't say anything about it."

"Of course not, because that's how you are." She gives me another quick hug. "Thank you. Seriously, you've saved her so much frustration and pain. Otherwise, she would've looked back and hated herself for missing the whole thing."

"You'd better go before I get all emotional."

She giggles. "Yeah, and I can't show up for my makeup with puffy eyes. Kylie will forgive a lot of things now, but I don't think she'd be cool with any of us ruining her pictures. Even me."

"Go, go. I need to get some writing done anyway. There are so many hours to kill."

"Don't forget to relax a little. We're flying home tomorrow afternoon."

As if I needed the reminder.

I don't want to waste a minute here. Really, I don't. But my brain is buzzing, and I know better than to squander this surge of creativity. I had a stellar night's sleep—the fact that there's hardly any oatmeal smeared on the pillowcase or in my hair is a testament to how thoroughly I passed out—and I feel refreshed and ready to go.

Besides, what would I do otherwise? Probably get a sunburn or something. Maybe break a bone for good measure. Give Sarah and her pals something to laugh themselves sick about.

Nope. I'm safer right here, on the patio, where the awning shades me from the sun and the sound of water lapping at the shore provides the perfect background noise.

Only …

The water's not lapping.

I look up from my screen at the realization. Normally, the water is gentle—okay, I don't know exactly what the water's like all the time, but over the past several days, it's been calming and peaceful.

Now? Not so much. There are waves—actual waves. It's starting to look pretty risky out there. I don't see many bathers willing to go farther out than knee height.

The sky's not so clear either with clouds piling up on the horizon.

Something tells me that Kylie's going to have more to deal with than puffy-eyed bridesmaids today.

Chapter Fourteen

Oh boy.

This had better be the fastest wedding in the history of weddings.

There isn't any rain yet, but there's quite a stiff breeze blowing. Breeze that's threatening to turn into full-blown wind.

And the sky isn't blue for the first time all week. It's a deep, menacing shade of gray with lots of angry clouds piled up on top of each other.

Yet here we are, all of us in our cute little chairs lined up in rows on either side of the long white runner. There are fifty guests in all, the rest of them having arrived late last night and this morning. There are floral arrangements on stands, one at the end of every row, and a beautiful arch just dripping in roses and orchids at the end of the runner.

It's a shame it looks like the palm trees in the distance are about to blow right over.

"Uh, this is looking dicey," somebody sitting near me says, like it needs to be said.

"I witnessed the rehearsal last night. It's a short ceremony."

That seems to ease a few minds, at least a little.

If they'd only get started, we might end up getting out of this with dry clothes and hair.

Once again, I wonder if it was worth getting all gussied up today. Two days in a row.

When the officiant steps up, standing under the arch, it looks like we're about to begin. Zack and his guys file in next to that spot, and soft music plays from carefully concealed speakers.

Thank goodness it's time to get this show on the road.

Kellen looks fantastic, needless to say, wearing the same seersucker suit the rest of the men in the party are wearing. That's one thing that surprises me about this, seeing as how Kylie wanted everything to be so fancy. Maybe she gave Zack a say in something after all.

Brandon walks his mom down the aisle before joining the rest of the groomsmen. He catches my eye, and I wink, making him smile. I hope we can spend more time together at the reception since there hasn't been much of a chance so far.

We all turn, expectant, waiting for the girls to file down the aisle. They're dressed identically in soft, flowy dresses the color of the sea beyond the ceremony site. Hayley's eyes look conspicuously watery when they meet mine, which of course gets me a little choked up.

No matter how big of a game she talks, she loves her sister. This means a lot to her.

The music changes, and we stand in response. I have to hold my arms at my sides to keep my dress from blowing around in what's less a breeze now and more of a wind. An increasingly steady wind.

Kylie smiles her way through it on the way down the aisle though, and I can't help but notice the way her eyes rarely leave Zack. She's finally in the moment. Remembering why she's here and why they're doing this.

I sneak a look over my shoulder at Zack in time to find him knuckling tears away before they can fall.

Oh gosh. My chest tightens along with my throat, and a familiar stinging sensation makes itself known behind my eyes.

What would it be like to be in her shoes right now? With the man I loved fighting back tears when he saw me in my wedding dress? To be so in love, so completely committed to another person, that I'd be willing to join my life with his in front of everybody who mattered to us?

And why is Kellen watching me watch Zack?

He offers a smile when our eyes meet. I wonder what he's thinking right now.

The officiant has to raise his voice over the rising wind. "It seems Mother Nature has something to say about this ceremony. She's just as excited over the soon-to-be newlyweds as the rest of us."

Get on with it. I'm biting my lip hard enough to hurt.

The air smells like rain—heavy, thick, wet. It's going to pour like all get-out in no time.

"We should proceed before things get any wilder out here." The poor guy is almost screaming now. "This beautiful occasion is in celebration of Kylie and Zack, two wonderful people I've had the honor of knowing for years. It brings me great joy to officiate over their union."

One of the pedestals holding a flower arrangement tips over in the wind, which sends a few guests seated near it scrambling to get out of the way. Kylie and Zack both look over, surprised. Kellen jumps into action to set it back on its base, though I feel it's a waste of time.

Nothing is going to be standing long in this wind.

"Kylie, do you take Zack—" The man's voice is cut off when a palm leaf smacks him in the face, but he recovers quickly enough.

A couple of the people on Zack's side scurry off to find shelter.

"Do you take Zack to be your lawfully wedded husband?" There's going to be a welt on the poor guy's face, but he's staying strong.

"I do!" Kylie's voice is loud, fierce. She's determined to get through this, even with hair escaping her carefully crafted updo. It's blowing around her face, though she's doing her best to tuck the loose strands behind her ears.

"And you, Zack. Do you take Kylie to be your

lawfully wedded wife?"

"I do!" Zack is squeezing Kylie's hands hard, like he's willing her to do this without her losing her mind.

Flowers are tearing loose all around them, flying in all directions.

Kellen steps in with the rings, which the couple exchange. There's no need for them to raise their voices anymore. We'd all like to hear it, but it's nearly impossible. All that matters is that they hear each other.

Kellen finds me, grimacing, and I know I must look the same as he does. Brokenhearted, hoping this is all over soon.

After all the work she put into this entire week too. None of it really mattered, not in the face of this disaster. Not when the exchanging of vows and rings and declaring their love to the world is what brought us all here in the first place. I'm sure she would have rather had it pour rain the rest of the week so long as today was beautiful.

Instead, it was the other way around.

The officiant raises his arms to signal the ceremony is over. "I now pronounce you husband and wife!"

And as if on cue, Mother Nature decides to congratulate the happy couple.

By pouring an absolute curtain of rain down on them and the rest of us.

Like, the kind of rain that makes it difficult to

see too far ahead. The kind of rain that drains everything of color. There's nothing in the world but gray clouds and walls of rain.

"Oh no!"

Just about everybody near me runs for cover, screaming and shrieking, but I know right away that there's no point in running. This is the sort of rain that soaks a person within moments, like a sudden before-and-after situation.

One second, dry. Coiffed. Made up.

The next? Drowned rat.

My heart is breaking for Kylie, who looks just as much like a drowned rat as I feel. All the girls are soaked, there are flowers blowing around in all directions and sticking to just about everything, and palm leaves are now whipping through the air at top speed.

A few empty chairs blow over. The arch sways back and forth until it finally falls backward and crashes to the ground.

Kylie and Zack are standing in the center of everything.

And Kylie is laughing. Like, laughing until she bends at the waist, one hand on her chest, gasping for air. Zack takes her by the arms and starts laughing, too, until they're leaning against each other for support.

Soon, the entire wedding party's in hysterics with two of the guys splashing around and throwing flowers at each other while the girls dance around with their bouquets raised overhead. Hayley throws her head back, arms stretched out to the sides, and I don't think I've ever seen her look so completely free and uncaring. Brandon finds her and sweeps her off her feet, swinging her in a circle and making her shriek with laughter.

It's perfect, in other words. Right down to the moment when Kylie and Zack take each other's faces in their hands, look into the other's eyes, and cement their union with a kiss.

I couldn't have come up with anything better if I wrote a thousand books.

And in the middle of it, Kellen's eyes find mine, and we smile.

The cherry on top.

Chapter Fifteen

I DON'T THINK this is the reception anybody had in mind.

But just like that disaster of a ceremony, it's perfect.

There won't be any pictures of the bridesmaids sitting around the bride with everybody's dresses arranged just so. And I sure hope the hair and makeup people got enough pictures of their work before the ceremony because not a single thing they did held up against the storm.

We've all since gone to our rooms to dry off and clean up. It seems most of us had at least one more nice outfit to wear for the reception, but that's not the case for everybody. For example, the people who only showed up this morning, who brought their wedding outfit and maybe something to wear while hanging out at the resort.

In other words, by the time we all gather in the banquet room, we are a real motley crew. There are khakis, capri pants, and even a couple of pairs of jeans. Then, there's me, wearing the dress I wanted to wear for last night's party—at least I'm getting some use out of it after all.

"Okay, I need to know." I pull Hayley aside and murmur in her ear, "Did somebody slip your sister a sedative today? No judgment if it was you."

She snickers, and we both look across the room. Kylie's hair is down, a mass of waves that makes her look like she just stepped out of the water. Then again, that's pretty much what she did after half-drowning out there. Her makeup is much more neutral than it was during the ceremony, before it got ruined. She's wearing a comfortable sundress and sandals.

And she's absolutely radiant. I've never seen her look more beautiful.

"If someone did, they deserve a great, big thank-you." But she scoffs just the same. "No, I think she's finally developed a sense of humor about this. I hope that doesn't change when she gets home; she could use a little easing up in her life in general."

"Yeah, I hope she doesn't forget."

She's basically survived what would break a lot of people—an absolute disaster on her wedding day. Her beautiful dress was ruined, and everything she'd spent so much money on was destroyed.

But she's smiling. Laughing. Hugging and dancing and living in the moment.

A man's voice rings in my ear. "Don't pretend to be modest about this. I think we both know who we have to thank."

Just knowing he's so close is enough to wake me

up from the inside out, making my blood hum, making my heart race. I can't hide a little smile as I look over my shoulder to find Kellen standing just behind me.

"Oh look, something else." Hayley makes her exit, leaving the two of us together.

"I'm not going to take credit for this, so don't even try. It was all up to Kylie. She chose to handle what happened today with grace."

"But you helped." His eyes are warm, sparkling. "Don't worry; I won't go around, accusing you of being full of yourself, if that's what you're concerned about."

"Listen, if I helped her feel even a little bit better this week, I'm satisfied with that."

He chuckles. "Fair enough. And you did; I know you did. I was there, remember?"

"Briggs!" Zack waves him over.

"Duty calls," I tease, though really, I would rather he stay with me. That would be selfish, wouldn't it? If I told him so? Even though it would be the truth. Is there anything wrong with being honest and letting him know how much I like being with him?

As usual, I'm so busy asking myself what to do that I lose the chance to do it. He is already on his way across the room, throwing his arms around his friend so somebody can take a picture of the two of them. There's real affection there, and I remember him mentioning how he promised that he would take it easy on the partying this week for the sake of being a good best man.

He spends a lot of time talking me up, making me sound like this great person, but he's the substantial one. Not me.

Okay, maybe me, too, but I'm not the only one. That's my point.

He has a way of jumbling my thoughts up, this guy.

"Come on. Let's dance." Brandon takes me by the hand and pulls me onto the floor, where even though dinner hasn't yet been served, people are already cutting loose and having a great time. Why not? Nothing about this day is going according to plan.

And if this wedding has taught me anything, it's to go with the flow. When things feel right, you just have to keep going. Don't ask yourself if you're making the right move. Don't scrutinize things too hard. Don't get caught up in the way things are supposed to be, the way you imagined them being, because guess what. Life almost never goes the way we planned it.

So, there's a choice to be made in those moments.

Either moan and complain and cry or dance.

I'm sure the staff is so glad Kylie is still happy that they would go along with just about anything at this point. Which is why the rest of the night is sort of scattered, relaxed. Dinner is served, and people meander back to their tables to eat. Kylie and Zack sit at a table by themselves, in full view of the rest of the room, with the wedding party surrounding them.

I'm supposed to be sitting alone—or at least at a table full of random stragglers who don't have dates. But things have already fallen to pieces when it comes to that with everybody pretty much deciding where they want to sit.

Kylie couldn't possibly care less, it seems, shrugging and waving her hands around. "Just make yourselves comfortable!"

To Hayley, that means taking me by the hand and pulling me across the room to her table. She was supposed to be sitting with the rest of the bridesmaids, but they've all scattered to sit with their other friends. Brandon has the chair to her left, and she points me to the one on her right.

"I don't belong over here!" I laugh, though that doesn't stop me from sitting down. I wasn't exactly looking forward to making small talk with a bunch of people I'd never met, who would have inevitably asked what I did for a living and then would have just as inevitably asked tons of invasive, embarrassing questions.

If I'd wanted invasive, embarrassing questions, I would've stayed home and spent the week with my grandmother.

"No such thing anymore." She shrugs before looking over my shoulder.

Something tells me I know what's about to happen before it actually does.

"This is much better than the seating arrangement Kylie came up with—no offense," Kellen says, looking at her brother and sister.

"Yeah, right, like I would take offense to that. I don't even think Kylie cares anymore." She gives him one of her most winning smiles. "Come on. Sit down."

As if I expected anything else.

As if she wasn't planning this in that devious little brain of hers.

But she's all innocent as Kellen sits next to me.

"Can I tell you a secret?" he murmurs, leaning in close to my ear.

"Of course, just don't expect me to keep it."

He laughs, and that, plus the look in his eyes, plus the scent of his cologne, is about enough to knock me out of my chair. "I liked it better out on your patio, when it was just the two of us."

"Funny, I was thinking the same thing." Though I look down at my hands with a wry grin. "I can do without the oatmeal treatment though."

"Okay, so the situation wasn't exactly perfect, but the company was."

"And look, I can even enjoy some wine without being afraid I'm going to fall out of my chair, unconscious." I even take a sip as if to prove my point.

He flashes a naughty grin. "Maybe I'll have to

get you drunk and have my way with you."

"You're all talk."

He arches an eyebrow as if he senses a challenge. "How so?"

"Last night would've been your chance to do that. And last I checked, the most you did was tuck me into bed."

"Oatmeal facials aren't my thing."

"Do me a favor and laugh or wink or something, so I know you're only kidding."

He does better. He picks up my hand and kisses the back, his breath hot against my knuckles as he laughs. "You know I'm only kidding. Once again, my sense of humor doesn't always translate."

Which is just as good of a time as any for the announcement to be made that it's time for toasts.

Meaning he has to get up and speak.

Maybe this wasn't the best moment for him to be reminded that his sense of humor doesn't always translate. Then again, maybe it was, seeing as how he now has to speak in front of a room full of people and might want to watch what he says.

I offer him a smile that I hope is encouraging before he stands, taking the microphone.

"Well," he sighs, "it's always nice to see a wedding go off without a hitch."

Which is exactly the right thing to say since everybody laughs warmly, raising their glasses in agreement.

He clamps a hand over Zack's shoulder, looking

down at him with a fond smile. "I remember the night these two met. Let's just say, Kylie has had an amazing effect on my best friend because, honestly, he was a walking disaster back then."

"Guilty!" Zack quips, earning another round of laughter.

"I remember thinking, as Zack went on and on about what a great girl he'd met, that he had never sounded that way about a girl before. Not ever. Not even when we were ten years old and he'd had a crush on the prettiest girl in our class."

He looks down at Kylie. "Don't worry; you're way hotter than she ever was."

Kylie laughs, leaning against Zack.

"Anyway, that was the first thing I thought. The second thing I thought—and forgive me for this, buddy—was that Kylie was way too good for him. Honestly, it's true," he insists, looking around the room when everybody laughs again. "I mean, not just physically—though I think we can all agree who we hope their children resemble, should the time ever come. She's brilliant, she's accomplished, and she's the kind of person you take seriously. A substantial person. That might sound old-fashioned, but it's probably the best compliment I can give, and there are very few people in the world who I would describe that way. And I had to wonder why she would give him the time of day since I'd known him since we were little kids, and I'll tell you, he's not that cool."

When the snickering dies down, he shrugs. "I guess she has a weakness for stray dogs and walking disasters. Because she looked at my best friend, who is like the brother I never had, and she saw through the shaggy hair cut and the jeans he'd been wearing since our freshman year of college. The person she saw underneath was worthy of her—at least, he had the potential to become worthy of her."

He squeezes Zack's shoulder. "And knowing him the way I do, I can promise you this. He'll spend the rest of his life working at becoming worthy of you. That, I don't doubt. You'll never find a better friend or a better partner than this guy. Not to mention the fact that you'll always look good in comparison to him."

Beautiful. He ends with one more laugh, through which more than a few people are sniffling and dabbing at their eyes.

"So, let's raise our glasses." Kellen holds up a champagne flute. "To Zack and Kylie, who've already shown us how well they can weather the storm together."

I can't help it. I'm dabbing at my eyes by the time he's finished too.

He's just one of those people. He finds a way to be charming and funny while stirring emotion. He's confident and comfortable, and he knows how to put those around him at ease.

In other words, he's pretty much perfect.

At least, that's how he looks in my eyes when he sits down next to me, miming the act of wiping sweat from his brow.

"Remind me to never do that again," he murmurs with a sigh of relief.

"Are you freaking kidding? That was awesome! I'm serious. I'd think you did this sort of thing professionally."

"Nah." He snickers, waving a hand. "Honestly, it helps that I really do like Kylie. And she's the person Zack needs in his life. In a big way."

Hayley and Brandon are at least pretending to pay attention to the speech being made by one of the bridesmaids, who has an entire three sheets of paper to read from.

I lean in to whisper in Kellen's ear to keep from interrupting, "You're just busting on him the way you guys have been doing all week."

He pulls back a little, eyes narrowing when he frowns. "No, I'm serious. She's turned his entire life around."

All right, this sounds like more than hyperbole. Looks that way, too, since he's stone-faced, and I'm suddenly embarrassed.

"Oh. I don't know anything about that. I figured you were kidding."

"No, he really went through some tough times a while back. He was getting in pretty deep."

I don't even know if I should be hearing this.

At the same time … okay, I'm more than a little

curious. Call it a natural part of my personality, that craving for a plot twist.

"In deep with what?"

He winces, his eyes moving back and forth, like he wants to be sure nobody hears us before whispering, "Gambling. We both dabbled in college. Betting on football and basketball games—you know, that sort of thing. Only he got deeper into it than I did. To the point where I thought he might need help, if you know what I mean."

"Oh my gosh. I had no idea."

"I guess he wants to keep it quiet. It makes sense, of course. I wouldn't want to blab about it to just anybody."

Right, but I'm a hundred percent sure I would've heard about this if Hayley had even the slightest clue, which she couldn't possibly. Which means, if Kylie knows, she's never told her family.

That makes sense now that I think about it, my mind spinning. She wouldn't want anybody to know things were less than perfect, would she? Always so dedicated to presenting a good front.

Though I have to wonder what she was thinking, wanting life to be perfect but getting herself involved with a gambler.

"If things were still bad for him, I doubt she would've married him. Right? She's a smart girl. She doesn't suffer fools, if you get what I mean."

His brow creases. "He's not a fool."

"I wasn't being literal." It's easy to forget sometimes that he can be very literal. "I'm only saying, she doesn't have a lot of patience with people who aren't as pulled together as she is."

He snorts, eyeing the bridesmaids now making slobbery, tear-filled speeches about what an amazing friend Kylie is and how their lives were forever changed when she stepped into them. "You sure about that?"

I see his point.

"I didn't mean to get you upset." He takes my hands, which were resting in my lap. "I'm sure you're right. Everything's fine with him now. He tells me so sometimes, you know."

"He does?" If anything, I don't know why he brought it up at all. I've never had that kind of addiction though. From what I've heard, it's not the sort of thing that ever goes away.

It's always there. The addict has to avoid falling back into the worst of it, is the thing.

So, it's probably always on his mind. He's got to stay vigilant.

"Especially during March Madness. He knows I'll always be checking on him. I can't not. I saw how bad things got. How low he sank. Bookies … well, you don't need to know all of it."

Frankly, I have to wonder if I needed to know any of it. Because, now, all I can do is hope Zack has things under control.

And that Kylie can manage to keep it a secret from her family, if it's still a secret at all.

"Finally," Hayley groans, tearing my attention away. "Time for dessert, and then we party."

Only I don't have such a big appetite for either dessert or dancing anymore since I know she'd hate it if I kept this from her.

Where's the line between being a good friend and leaving a man's past alone?

Chapter Sixteen

"I UPSET YOU earlier."

I shake my head with a smile. "You didn't."

It's a lie. Kellen upset the heck out of me. Now that I know about Zack's issue, I can't think about anything else.

It's not the worst thing a person can be guilty of, of course, and I know it. He's not a murderer. He isn't violent. He's a good man. And he adores Kylie.

But she's worked so hard. Call it an overactive imagination, a by-product of having read so many books over the course of my life, but I can't help but imagine him going through her savings someday.

No matter how smart she is, love has a way of blinding people to fundamental truths.

"Because, really, there's no other excuse for a beautiful woman to frown so much when she's in my arms and I'm taking her on a trip around the dance floor." Kellen's arm tightens around my waist.

Giggling, I ask, "You're sure that's the only reason a girl would frown when she's in your arms? You have a pretty high opinion of yourself."

The shoulder under my left hand shrugs. "You tell me whether it's a high opinion or whether it's fact. Don't pretend you aren't swooning over my awesome dance moves."

"We're swaying back and forth. A toddler can sway back and forth in time with the music."

"And I haven't stepped on your feet once yet, have I?"

I lean against him, laughing. He doesn't seem to mind.

"That's more like it. It's our last night together, and I would hate for you to be sad."

Well, if he doesn't want me to be sad, he could start with not saying things like that.

It takes serious effort not to react badly. To keep from reacting at all. "Our last night together?" It's not easy, talking with a lump in my throat.

This isn't how I wanted things to go.

Though I guess I shouldn't have assumed anything. I told myself I wouldn't, didn't I? I wouldn't let myself get tricked into believing there was more here than a weeklong acquaintance. A little fun. Flirting.

So, why do I feel like I'm going to cry?

"Our last night here, yeah. Unless you know something I don't know." He pulls his head back, searching, trying to catch my eye even though my head is ducked.

I would rather he didn't see my face. I don't want to imagine what a nerd he'd think I was if he put two and two together.

"No, tonight's the last night."

"I mean, seeing you in the city won't be the same as it is here, will it?"

And here I am, with my heart soaring. *Darn it! Why am I so easily swayed?*

It could be because he's such an exceptional person. The sort of man a girl could be attracted to. To want to know better than a week at a resort would allow.

"So, you want to get together back home?" *Did I sound cool when I said that?* I hope I did. That's what I'm going for, though, historically, my moments of coolness have been few and far between.

Hayley knows all about that.

"Am I wrong? Do you not want to?" He looks at me again. "I've made mistakes before. There I go again, thinking I'm charming and funny and not too hard on the eyes ..."

"Shut up."

"So, is that a yes? Yes, you'll see me in New York? Yes, you'll have dinner with me?"

I could practically float off the floor. If it wasn't for him holding on to me the way he is, I just might. "Yes. It's a yes."

"Whew! I thought I was gonna have to start begging."

Our eyes meet. I'm so happy; I couldn't wipe the smile from my face if I tried. Though what's the point of trying? Why bother pretending to be anything less than thrilled and relieved and, yes, flattered?

"I wasn't sure you wanted to see me after this," I admit with a flush on my cheeks. "I mean, no pressure. I don't expect anything."

"Don't sell yourself short. And know when to leave well enough alone," he adds with a twinkle in his eye. "Otherwise, you'll end up talking your way out of getting asked out."

"I'll have to keep that in mind."

The song changes, though it's still slow. Romantic. The lights are lower than they were before, casting a soft amber glow over the room, which the candles and glinting crystal decor only add to.

We might as well be in a dream—except there are eyes staring daggers at my back, which doesn't happen when I'm dreaming. People actually like me in my dreams. Bridesmaids don't usually hate me in my dreams.

Let them. Let them see I've won the best man this week. For once, I don't mind showing off a little.

Kellen leans in until his lips nearly brush against my ear. "Though I don't take rejection easily, you know. Some people would call me downright stubborn."

"You?" I snort. "The man who barged into the kitchen and demanded oatmeal? Who strong-armed his way into my room last night, whether I wanted you there or not?"

"For your own good."

"Hmm." I snort. "According to whom? Maybe I'll be busy when we get back to the city."

"Every night?"

"I'll find something to do."

Our eyes meet, and I can tell he knows I'm only kidding. Though it's partly a joke, partly the truth. I don't like being told what to do, which is something he's going to need to get used to if he wants to date for real.

"Got it." His smile widens. "You should know, I love a challenge."

"So do I."

There might as well not be anybody else here but the two of us. That's how it's been all night. Talking, eating together, dancing. I should try to enjoy time with Hayley, too, right?

I can't imagine having anywhere close to as good of a time without him. Even with my best friend in the whole world.

Besides, something tells me she'd find a way to leave me with Kellen anyway. One of her patented getaways.

"Would it be completely shitty if I asked if I could walk you back to your room tonight?"

My face is maybe a few seconds away from bursting into flames. Not because I'm embarrassed. Not even close.

More like I've been wondering if he would ask. Hoping he would ask.

There's nothing quite like getting exactly what you want and wondering what the heck to do with it.

I mean, not that I have to wonder exactly. *But would it be completely cliché to sleep with the best man tonight?*

What's wrong with being cliché every once in a while?

I can practically hear Maggie's voice in my head, asking that question. It's uncanny. And a real turn-off, but that's beside the point.

I'm taking too long to give him an answer. I know I am. I can tell by the way his face falls an inch at a time.

"It would be shitty," he finally mutters.

"No, no, no." I slap a hand to my forehead. "I'm such a dork. Of course I want that. It's just that I think too much. I overthink until I miss opportunities I don't want to miss."

His eyelids slide down partway, like shades over a window. His mouth lifts at one corner. "Tonight's a new start for the newlyweds. Maybe it can be a new start for you too. Something new. Going with your gut. Doing what feels right in the moment without overthinking it. What do you say?"

What do I say?

I say, forget dancing.

I say, it's time to get out of here.

I back away with a wink, his hand in mine, and

lead him from the dance floor. It's been a long night anyway, and the party's starting to wind down. Now's as good a time as any to make our escape.

Hayley catches my eye as we leave the banquet room and can't conceal a grin. I only scowl at her for immediately jumping to the conclusion she jumped to.

Granted, she's not exactly wrong, but still. Just because we're going back to the room doesn't mean we're going to take our clothes off or anything like that.

But dang, wouldn't it be a shame if we didn't? Talk about a wasted opportunity.

"Wow. You'd never know there was a storm."

The sky has cleared, moon and stars shining. Like nature said everything it wanted to say all at once and got it over with rather than lingering and drawing things out.

That would account for the unbelievable strength of the storm anyway. I can't remember seeing anything like that in my entire life. At least, I had never been in the middle of such a storm before.

"It's not just that. Everything's cleaned up," Kellen notices, pointing here and there. No palm leaves strewn around, no overturned lounge chairs. "They know what they're doing around here, for sure."

"I'll miss this place," I admit. "Corny, I know. But I will. I've never been anywhere like this before."

"I thought your grandmother was super rich and lived on Park Avenue though. You mean, she doesn't live a wealthy life?"

I'm so taken aback by this that it stops me short. He's surprised when he finds that I'm frozen in place, turning to me with a frown.

"How did you know about my grandmother?"

He blinks hard, fast. "You told me about her. Don't you remember? On the bus."

Of course. For the second time in maybe fifteen minutes, I have no option but to slap my forehead. "I'm sorry. Right. I told you about her and my parents and everything."

"Hey." He draws me closer, hooking a finger under my chin and tipping my head up so we're face-to-face and barely an inch apart. "Did somebody hurt you? Or try to anyway? Why are you suspicious when someone thinks you're incredible?"

Have I been hurt? There's a laugh.

"After a certain age, doesn't everybody have their scars?"

"I guess so. You'd have to live in a bubble if you wanted to keep from getting hurt." He takes a deep breath and slowly lets it out while his eyes search my face. "I can't imagine anybody wanting to hurt you, Kitty Valentine. They'd have to be heartless."

"You might be amazed."

He offers a tiny, sad smile before catching my

mouth with his, and I can't remember ever being hurt a day in my life.

It's a sweet kiss. Tender, gentle.

That doesn't keep my nerve endings from jumping and sizzling. It's like this past week has been prolonged foreplay—teasing, bantering, getting to know each other.

Now, all that tension has broken, and there's nothing but relief. The sort of relief that makes my knees weak, to where I have to hold on to him or risk folding into a heap.

He holds me up, arms tight around me. He won't let me fall.

My hero.

Chapter Seventeen

"I HOPE YOU don't think I'm this sort of girl all the time." Missy glanced over her shoulder, watching as Trent put his clothes on. Boxers. Pants. Shirt.

It was almost sad really. Him covering himself up. He was too delicious to be clothed all the time. The most perfect man she'd ever seen in person.

And definitely the most perfect she'd ever had the pleasure of touching. Tasting. Feeling.

She could remember the taste of his skin under her lips, under her tongue. The sound of his heavy breathing against her ear, hot on the skin of her neck.

And other places. So many places. He'd taken his time getting to know her body, though he'd seemed to instinctively know what she liked. What she needed.

How long had it been since she'd been taken good and hard, until there was nothing to do but scream her approval?

The memory made her mouth go dry.

Why couldn't she control herself for just a little while, until he was out of the room and it was safe to fall back on the bed and pick through every last memory?

Probably because he'd just given her a night like she

had never known before. Sweeter. More passionate.

The kind of night a woman could get addicted to if she wasn't careful.

And Missy had spent so, so long being careful. Painfully careful.

She didn't want to be that way anymore.

Yet there she was, saying stupid things. Like this was some mid-twentieth-century movie or show where the girl had just lost her innocence and hoped the boy would still respect her in the morning.

It had been a long time since Missy was innocent.

Still, somehow, this felt different. Deeper. More real.

More dangerous, too, because of all that.

"You're not?" His hair stuck up in all directions. He ran his fingers through it, combing it down. Fingers she could remember being on her. Inside her.

A flush burned her cheeks at the memory. "No, I'm not."

"That's disappointing because I like this sort of girl."

"Stop."

He laughed. It wasn't a taunt, a tease. He wasn't treating her like a joke. How did she know? No way of telling. She felt it just the same.

"Hey. Not everything has to be so serious." He sat next to her, where she had just about wrapped herself in an entire cocoon of sheets. "No, I don't think you're a slut, if that's what you're trying to say. Even if you were, that's none of my business. Don't be so worried about what people think about you."

"I'm not worried about people in general." She found the courage to look him in the eye. "Just about certain

people whose opinion matters."

"My opinion matters?"

She managed a soft laugh. "I told you, I'm not that sort of girl. Which means you must be something special, right?"

He kissed her shoulder. Even that simple, touch was as tender as any caress she could imagine. "That means more than I can say. Thank you."

"You're welcome."

"No, I mean it." He turned her head, so she faced him, and then buried his hand in her hair. Hair he had run his hands through, had clutched in his fists. His touch was softer now. "I'm not good at things like that. These moments, you know. I haven't had many of them. Wanting to spend time with a woman afterward. Staying in bed. Sitting here, making sure she was okay with what we did."

He looked away before she did, making her wonder how much more uncomfortable he had to be than she was. Even she'd had the nerve to hold his gaze.

Maybe it was one thing to pretend to be comfortable with himself and another to truly okay inside.

In a way, this was just as new to him as it was to her.

I sit back, reading over what I just wrote and remembering the moments that had inspired it.

Kellen hadn't stayed until morning the way Trent did in the book. Missy wasn't sharing a room, but I am. Hayley had been nice enough to give us time to be alone and might have stayed away all night if I hadn't told her it was okay to come back.

Am I writing the scene this way because this is how I wish it had gone? I think so.

It's been almost a week since we got back from the resort, and my tan is still going strong, so that's a good thing.

Matt's left me alone. I'm not sure what to make of that. He's such a baby, sulking in his apartment. I know he's in there too. I know he's alive and well.

How do I know?

The fact that a girl spent half the night moaning his name. He's up to his old tricks, apparently. There I was, spoiled all this time. Enjoying silence while working in the middle of the night.

I didn't bother playing the marching band music. It would've been petty, and while I am many things, I don't like to imagine myself as being petty.

Not to mention the fact that I'm suspicious of him. What if he was trying to goad me into confronting him? What if he wanted that to be our first contact after so long?

I wasn't about to fall for that trick. If that was what he had in mind anyway.

Not that I'm exactly going to ask if that was what he had in mind because I don't want to make it look like I'm overthinking it and—oh shoot, I'm driving myself nuts. I should get back to thinking about work.

With my elbows on the desk, I rest my chin in my hands and read over again what I have so far.

How can I capture the way I felt when he left me

there, in the room, and I wished it hadn't felt like I was saying good-bye to him for good?

No, I never told him I wasn't that kind of girl. Even I know how hopelessly silly that sounds. It's one thing for a character in a book to come up with something like that, but me?

At least he stuck around for a little bit afterward. That was nice. We walked along the beach for a while before he headed back to his room to get packed.

Now?

I need to get my head fully into work, so I won't be tempted to check the phone again. And again.

So what if he hasn't gotten in touch with me yet? So what if there hasn't even been a text message?

So what if I'm starting to wonder whether I was right in the first place? That he only wanted to get in my panties while we were at the resort and then disappear in the night? I guess he never had any intention of us going to dinner or doing anything else once we were back from the wedding.

And I need to be okay with that, which is why I've decided to put him behind me.

While writing a book based on our experiences. I swear, it's like I've decided to live the rest of my life in purgatory. Punishing myself, serving my time before going on to something better. Something less torturous.

I know what I need to do with my book at least. That much I can control. I'll have Trent avoid Missy, though it'll be for completely innocent reasons. Death in the family or something equally unpreventable.

If I were Missy, what would I do?

Oh, to hell with that. I am Missy, let's be honest. And what I would love to do is go to him and ask who he thinks he is. Why he thought it would be okay to lie to me. Six days, and he hasn't bothered to get in touch?

I reached out to him. The ball is completely in his court.

Yes, I'll have Missy confront Trent to his face. Let her take him down a peg or two.

When did I start crying?

I have to go to the bathroom to rinse my face before taking a long, hard look at myself in the mirror. I don't look any different than usual. My skin is tanner than normal, but that's not saying much, considering I'm normally pale enough to be nearly transparent.

There's no sign on my forehead reading, *Sucker*.

It must be something I transmit via unspoken signal or something. A chemical that men can smell and translate as me being a pushover. Easy to get to. Easy to sweet-talk and then crumple up like a candy wrapper and throw away.

I am not that person. I'm not that girl.

I'm Kitty freaking Valentine.

And none of this pep-talking keeps me from jumping on my ringing phone like it's a live grenade about to go off and there are people around me whose lives I'm trying to save.

"Oh, it's you," I mumble, dropping onto the sofa in a breathless heap after answering.

"Hello to you too." Hayley laughs. "What's up? Stuck on a scene?"

"Yeah, I'm stuck. The juices aren't flowing."

"I'm sorry. Maybe you should get out and take a walk. Or, hey, go up and sit on the roof. It's a gorgeous day, which I only wish I were able to enjoy instead of being stuck in the office. But you know how it is. I took a week off, God forbid, so I need to keep my head down and be a good girl for a while."

No, I don't know how it is. Not personally. Only through what she's told me. With all things being equal, I like my job a lot better than hers.

"I think the roof is off-limits for me right now. I might end up running into somebody I'd rather not see. And I'm sure he doesn't want to see me either."

"You still haven't seen Matt? I swear, the two of you are worse than children. Do you need me to come in and mediate? Should we have a sit-down?"

"Shush."

"No, I mean it. Obviously, I can't count on the two of you to act like adults and work your shit out rationally. You need to be guided into this."

"You're ridiculous."

"Says the girl who refuses to speak to her neighbor because he was mean to her."

"There's a line, babe. Your toe is on it." I have to clench my teeth against anything else that wants to come out.

"Okay, sorry. But I do think it's a shame you two aren't talking. That's all I'm gonna say."

"I'm a little more concerned about not talking to somebody else right now, to be honest with you." Just imagining his face in my head makes my chest hurt. Especially when I see him poised over me …

"He still hasn't called you back?"

"I would've told you if he had."

"Oh, honey, I'm sorry. Do you want me to reach out to Kylie and see if Zack knows anything?"

It's tempting. Oh-so tempting. That would be simple, wouldn't it? Having Kylie find out for me. She owes me just slightly, doesn't she? I did save her entire wedding experience and all that.

Yes, I know I didn't want to take too much credit for that, but times have changed. I'm emotional now. I'm feeling dumped and used.

"No," I sigh once the angel and devil on my shoulders stop fighting it out. "No, she shouldn't do that. The girl just got married a week ago, and knowing her, she's probably fixated on her next project by now. Like world domination."

"Who knows? Maybe she's taken her new relaxed attitude and decided to make it a lifelong thing. Maybe next time I visit her apartment, I won't feel like I'm walking into a Pinterest ad."

"You know what I hope? That she drops those

girlfriends of hers for good. She deserves better than that."

"I hope you're right. Maybe I'll put a bug in her ear about that one instead of one about you and Briggs."

"Don't say his name, please. I feel like such an idiot. He told me we were going to go out once we were back home. He could've just said no. Heck, I might still have slept with him. Who knows?"

"There might be something wrong. He's not that kind of person. I'll look into it."

"Don't."

"Too late!" She's off the call before I can beg her to please not make a bigger fool out of me than I've already made out of myself.

I mean, she'd have to work pretty hard to do that after all. I wouldn't want to take up her valuable time.

Chapter Eighteen

ENOUGH OF THIS *nonsense.*

I've paced the entire length of my apartment so many times that my legs are tired.

I've rearranged the books on the shelves, which now sit in order by author and then by title. I don't think I like it, and I'll probably change things up again soon, but for now, they'll have to sit.

I might resort to scrubbing the bathroom soon.

Eek. Anything's better than that.

Which is what sends me up the narrow staircase and onto the roof. It's an absolutely glorious day and well past the time when Matt normally finishes working. I heard his door open and close a few minutes ago, followed by the door at the other end of the hall, which leads up to the roof.

Might as well get this over with. Even if he's still mad, I doubt he'll throw me over the ledge.

Though I might want to send Hayley a message to warn her, just in case they find my body on the sidewalk. Somebody ought to know my last movements, if they are indeed my last.

No, I'm usually the one threatening grievous

bodily harm. Matt would rather taunt me half to death.

There he is, sitting in his chair, a small cooler next to him. The light from the late afternoon sun hits him in just such a way that his brown hair now looks flecked with red and gold. His back is to me, but I know from the tightening of his shoulders that he heard me step out from the stairwell.

Without saying a word, I go to the spot under the ledge where my chair is tucked and pull it out before plopping down not far from him. My normal position.

As usual, he opens the cooler and pulls out a bottle of beer, popping the cap before extending his arm in my direction. A good sign.

It might be the level of emotion I'm running at right now, but that simple gesture is enough to choke me up. I gladly accept the beer without saying a word.

For a while, it's enough for us to sit in silence.

Though he doesn't stay silent for long.

"So, what finally made you decide to come up here?" He glances my way from the corner.

I hold up the beer bottle. "What do you think? It was your turn to buy the beer, and I didn't want to give you the chance to back out on me."

"You came up here because you love my beer so much?"

"You have decent taste in beer. Accept one of the few compliments I've ever given you."

"Fair enough." He takes a pull from his bottle before asking, "Why are you really here?"

"You are exhausting."

"Is that why?"

"No, dummy. It's because I got tired of avoiding you. It's easier to exist without wondering if I'm gonna end up running into you in the hallway and seeing your stupid face. And what'll happen if we do run into each other."

As an afterthought, I add, "I miss Phoebe too. I've been wanting to see her all week."

"She's been scratching at the door, trying to get to you. And I practically have to drag her into the apartment when I bring her in from a run. She'd rather be at your place."

"Gee, I can't imagine why. Maybe because I'm so much nicer to be around than you."

"Oh yeah, she told me that."

"Shut up."

"Fine, don't believe me." He finishes his beer before taking another. "So, how was the wedding?"

"Honestly, it was great. It really was." I have to give it a moment's thought before continuing, "I mean, yeah, there was a massive storm in the middle of the ceremony and we all got soaked and the officiant almost got his face knocked off by a flying palm leaf, but yeah, it was great."

He almost spits out his beer. "You're kidding. So, you said it was great, but that's what happened?"

"I know it sounds nutty, but honestly, the whole thing turned out perfectly. They were …" A sigh escapes me, one I didn't know I had been holding inside until I heard it. "They were so happy. And so in love. Which is what made it perfect."

"Sometimes, I forget you're a romantic at heart."

"Sometimes, I forget you're a cynical pain in the butt. And you could maybe try not to sound so dismissive when you say that, by the way. Like there's something wrong with me for being a romantic."

He winces. "I didn't mean it like that. I didn't expect you to take it that seriously."

"Yes, well, words mean something. When you say them, they mean something. You can't throw them around and expect people not to care."

He's quiet for a while, though I can tell he's studying me from his chair. I won't favor him with a look in his direction.

"Why do I feel like this isn't entirely about what's happening right now? Between you and me in this moment?"

"I don't know." I shrug.

"Because, yeah, it's been a while since we've hung out, but you don't usually get so wounded. You can give as good as you get. I've spent all these days girding my loins, waiting for you to flay me with a few well-chosen words and the threat of … I don't know … throwing something at me."

"I guess things have changed. I don't, um …"

Another sip of beer doesn't help me clear my head any. Not that I expected it to. It's more a stalling tactic, so I can figure out what to say. "I don't have a lot of patience right now."

"What's wrong? For real. Straight up. One friend to another."

One friend to another. Right. This is going to involve swallowing a whole lot of pride. I hope I don't choke on it.

"Things haven't been going very well with the person I was telling you about. The one who I was supposed to date for the sake of my next book."

"Okay."

I almost wish he would say something else. Then again, if he said much more, I'd probably wish he'd mind his own business.

"He's ghosting me."

"What a dick."

"Stop." I roll my eyes at him with a disgusted expression.

"I'm serious. I've never ghosted a woman, and I never will. It's lame and cheap and pathetic. Like, be a man. Grow a pair. If you don't want to go out with somebody, fucking tell them."

His support gives me added confidence.

I sit up a little straighter in the chair. "Right? That's what I'm saying! But, no, he went out of his way to make sure I thought he wanted to see me when the wedding was over."

His eyes narrow. "You fucked him."

"Ew! You jerk!"

"You did. Admit it."

"Why are you like this?"

"Because it's obvious, and I have a talent for seeing the obvious. You slept with him, and now, he's ghosting you. And that hurts, and, yeah, of course it does. He's an asshole for doing that. Men are pigs."

"Shut up," I whisper, though it's with a tiny smile.

"I'm serious. We're a plague upon the world and deserve to be dragged outside and shot. All of us, all at once."

"Shut up for real."

"I'm just saying." He grins a little, which gets me grinning. "I'm sorry. Really. Very sorry. The guy's an asshole. But, hey, there could be a genuine reason for it."

"Don't do that. It's so much harder when I tell myself those things. It's easier for me to let it go."

"Okay, sue me. I was trying to be a friend."

The thing is, I know he was. Which is why I let it go without arguing any further. "At least I can give us a happy ending in the book. My hero is a good guy. He wouldn't use a girl for a night and disappear."

"That's how it should be."

"And that's why I write romance. It's the way things should be. Happily ever after and all that. Genuine intentions, misunderstandings, the couple getting together in the end once everything's been worked out."

"But you don't want to believe that's possible for you in real life?"

I can only shrug with a sad smirk. "Real life doesn't work that way. We wouldn't need romance books as an escape otherwise."

"Oof. I'm not used to this version of Kitty. I'm used to, you know, rainbows and unicorns and sarcasm Kitty. Witty-banter Kitty."

"This is the Kitty I am right now."

It's hilarious really, that he appears to give this serious thought. He stares at his bottle and starts picking at the label, his brow furrowed.

Finally, he nods. "That's cool. You can be whoever you are."

"Thank you for granting me permission to be who I am."

"Ah, there she is." He throws me a wink and a smirk. "You look like you got a lot of sun. That's good anyway. I'm jealous. This is as much sun as I've been afforded lately."

He stretches his long legs out in front of him, and not for the first time do I wonder why he walks around the roof barefoot. The man is just begging for an infection.

"Working too hard?"

"The market's volatile right now. I've been watching it like a hawk. Not much time for stepping onto the roof with a beer—or for much of anything else."

"Hmm." I can't help it. "Seems to me there was time for at least one other thing recently."

He snorts. "Yeah, well, there's always time for that."

"Good to know you have your priorities in order."

"Always."

"Because men are pigs?" I raise an eyebrow before polishing off my beer.

"Something like that."

I'm still grinning when my phone rings. Darn my treasonous heart for skipping a beat, hoping it's Kellen. Hoping this has all been a misunderstanding, just like in one of my books.

"Hayley," I whisper for Matt's benefit.

"Don't let me stop you."

He makes no move to give me privacy. Why would he? Such a pain.

Hayley's breathless when I answer the call. "I'm gonna swing by in a car in, like, ten minutes. I got ahold of Kylie. There's a big problem. We're going to the hospital."

Chapter Nineteen

I CAN'T HELP but go through flashbacks of rushing into the ER when Grandmother had her heart attack. It's barely been six months since that awful night.

This isn't quite as dire. Though my heart is still in my throat as I hurry into the hospital with Hayley at my side.

"Did Kylie say what happened?"

"No. Just that he was hurt pretty badly."

Could she be a little vaguer?

"Was it a car accident?"

"I don't know. But he's been here for the past two days, so it must be bad." We get on the elevator, and she pushes the button for his floor. "Zack's been here since he found out."

I can barely keep myself from jumping out of my skin as we ride up to Kellen's floor. Here I was, blaming him for not getting in touch with me, while he was lying in a hospital bed.

I'm glad now that Hayley reached out to her sister even though I'd begged her not to.

Kylie is waiting in the hallway, sitting on what

looks like a pretty uncomfortable plastic chair. "Hey," she whispers, hugging both of us. "It'll be okay. He woke up a little while ago."

"He was unconscious all this time?" I can hardly breathe. Hayley has to put an arm around me for support.

Kylie nods. Her eyes are red-rimmed. "He was unconscious when he was brought in and then they found internal bleeding so they took him into surgery and were able to stop the bleeding. He's been in and out since he woke from the surgery. They banged him up pretty badly."

They.

They?

Who's they?

I look to Hayley, who clearly picked up on her sister's choice of words, just like I did.

"*They* banged him up? What are we talking about here?"

"I imagined it was a car accident or something," I add.

Kylie's bronzed skin goes white. "Oh. Right." She runs her hands through her hair, either distracted or nervous. I'd bet on the latter.

"What happened to him?" I whisper even though I'm not sure I want to know now. Not when the little bit of information I've been given makes me sick to my stomach. *How much worse will it be when I find out the rest of it?*

She looks from me to Hayley and back again. I

can tell she doesn't want to say, which only drives me half-crazy with the need to know more.

Hayley's legal mind is already turning. "Will it incriminate him in something if he admits what happened? Will it put either of us in jeopardy?"

Kylie frowns, shaking her head. "I don't think so."

"Wait." Now, I'm thoroughly confused, like I walked into a movie halfway through. "What would he be involved in that could be so serious?"

And why didn't Kylie act stunned when Hayley said that?

Instead, she took the questions in stride and answered as best she could.

Poor Kylie.

She glances in the direction of Kellen's room, chewing her lip. "It's more like I don't think he wants it blabbed about. He's ashamed. I know he wouldn't want you to think badly of him. He couldn't stop talking about you to Zack the morning after the wedding. He was looking forward to seeing you again. This is going to crush him."

Crush him? What about me?

One look at Hayley tells me she's no more aware of the ins and outs than I am, though she's concerned. "If he wanted to continue seeing Kitty, this is something she would've found out about eventually. What is he hiding?"

Kylie rubs her temples. "Okay. You're right. You would've found out anyway—I mean, I would've seen to it. As it was, I had my reservations, but I figured I wouldn't say anything about it until I knew the two of you were going to continue seeing each other. No sense in bringing it up if you'd left things back at the resort. And, really, if it wasn't for him and Zack being so close, I might've said something anyway. But Zack is super protective of him."

"Protective of what exactly?" I'm ready to explode at this point. I just might unless I get answers.

She takes a deep breath and lowers her voice even further. "Briggs is a compulsive gambler. It's an addiction. It started back in college."

It hits me with the force of a bomb going off in my face.

Yet my first reaction isn't one of surprise. Or dismay.

It's incredulity.

"No. That's not right. He told me ..." I can't go on.

"What did he tell you?"

Now, I don't know whether or not I should say, but with the two of them looking at me the way they are, it seems like the time to keep my mouth shut has passed. "He told me Zack was the one with a problem."

Her brow lowers. "Oh, he said that, did he? Well, he lied. Yes, I knew that Zack had bet on games in college, but he stopped very quickly once he saw how deeply Briggs had fallen into it.

Apparently, there was some trouble with loan sharks—Zack would never go into detail—but things got bad when Briggs's family found out. He supposedly cleaned up his act after that—at least, that's what he told Zack whenever he checked on him."

The world is spinning around me.

Kellen created an entire story—no, actually, that isn't true. He just flipped the truth, making himself look like the good friend and Zach the gambler, when in truth, he's a really shitty friend. I suppose addiction will do that to you.

"Here. Sit." Hayley nudges me toward one of the chairs positioned against the wall. I have no choice but to lower myself into it.

She turns to her sister, still holding my hand. "What you're saying is, Briggs owed people money, and they beat him up when he didn't have it."

"In a nutshell, yes." Kylie touches my shoulder. "I know it must be hard to hear. I'm sorry. We really did hope he had himself back on track."

My head bobs up and down without my meaning to move it. "I understand. And I feel like I owe you both an apology, too. I went round and round with myself wondering if I should say something about it to you or Hayley."

"Don't feel guilty," Kylie says. "I understand why you wouldn't want to bring it up at my wedding. I should have told Hayley not to push you two together and why."

"No kidding." Hayley snorts.

"It's not your fault," I remind her, looking up. "I don't hate Kellen. I feel sorry that he got into this mess. He's a nice person. I like him so much."

Kylie sits next to me. "I know it would mean a lot for him to hear you say that, though nobody would ever force you to go and talk to him. I don't know if he'd even want to face you right now. Not only because he's banged up. He's also embarrassed."

"I can understand that."

Zack steps out of the room, looking surprised to find us there. He stares at his wife, who shrugs.

"They were worried. Hayley asked me if I knew what was going on with him. I couldn't pretend not to know."

He looks from Hayley to me. "It doesn't matter now, I guess. This isn't something you can hide from people you care about. I keep trying to tell him that, but … well, it's too late now. You were bound to find out."

"I'm just glad she found out when she did." Hayley's touch is protective, just like the fierceness in her voice.

I know her heart's in the right place. Truly, I do.

That doesn't stop me from feeling slightly irritated. "I'm okay, we didn't make each other any promises. It doesn't matter. Not for my sake. I feel sorry for him. Not for me."

"I'm always going to worry more about you

than I do about anybody else. That's just how it is." She shrugs.

Looking at Zack, I feel guilty for ever having believed the story Kellen told me about him. But I still wonder why he lied about it all.

I don't know what hurts more, honestly. I never gave him any reason to make up a story. I never asked anything from him.

Except for him to be truthful with me.

Sure, I never came right out and spoke those words aloud, but did I need to? Isn't it sort of implied?

Zack ducks back into Kellen's room, and I hear murmuring coming from inside. I know what Zack's doing. What I don't know is whether or not I want to see Kellen. Especially if he's banged up badly. I'm not sure if I can handle it.

There's too much going through my head and my heart. I'm not sure what to think or whether I need to think of anything at all.

He doesn't owe me anything. I don't owe him anything.

Actually, that's not quite right. He owes me an explanation.

But I'm not so sure I need them right this very minute. The man's in a hospital bed and just got through surgery. The last thing he needs to do is explain himself.

Clearly, he feels otherwise since, when Zack sticks his head out the door and into the hall, he murmurs, "Briggs wants to see you."

"You don't have to," Hayley whispers. "You really don't."

"I know." But I stand just the same and throw my shoulders back.

If nothing else, he needs a friend right now. I can do that much.

I think.

Chapter Twenty

THE FIRST THING I notice when entering the room is the number of machines all around. That's not such a surprise. I saw them when I was here with Grandmother.

The second is the mass of swollen flesh that used to be Kellen's face.

I mean, it's still Kellen's face. But now, it has stitches in it. A swollen eye. A split lip.

I can barely breathe. I wish I hadn't come in here. I wish I hadn't come to the hospital.

I wish I could've let this entire thing go—from Kellen and his promises to everything that happened at the resort.

But of course, that's not how life works. We can't go back, and there's no way of knowing how things will turn out. All we can do is the best we can do.

His good eye opens. "Hey." His voice is weak. I guess that's understandable.

"Hey," I say, taking a seat next to him.

"You're still as pretty as you were back there." He tries to smile, but it's not easy with his face the way it is. I see pain in his eye, the way he winces. "I wish I could say the same for myself."

"You don't look that bad."

"You're a terrible liar."

"You would know. You're better at it than I am."

He slowly blows out a long sigh. "I deserve that."

Whether or not he thinks he deserved it, I feel like garbage for saying it. "I'm sorry. It was uncalled for."

"No, it was called for. And more than that. But maybe you can have a little sympathy for a guy after he had his insides opened up today."

I touch his hand. "Kellen, I'm so sorry."

"No more than me." He looks away, up at the ceiling. "I knew I wasn't good enough for you the whole time. I should've discouraged you. I should've acted like an asshole and driven you away. I was wrong. I was weak, the way I've always been."

"Don't say that. You aren't weak."

"You don't have to be nice. You don't owe me anything."

My fingers close over his anyway. "What I don't understand is why you made up that story about Zack. Why go out of your way to lie like that?"

"Don't you get it?" He snorts. "No, I guess not. I wanted to see how you'd react. What you would say. You don't know what it's like to have something like this inside you. Carrying it around all the time. Knowing people wouldn't think about you the same way if they knew the truth."

"So, you pretended the situation was reversed and Zack was the one with the problem in order to test me?"

"Don't put it that way, please."

"But you were. I guess I must've passed, huh?"

Another sigh. "You're tough."

"You already knew that." I won't apologize this time.

"I can only ask you to forgive me. Don't hate me too much."

"I don't hate you. I'm sad for you, more than anything."

"Shit, that's worse."

I know he's trying to joke, but I hear the truth underneath just the same. Nobody wants to be pitied, especially somebody with a lot of pride. "Sorry. That sounded bad."

"Nah. You're a good person. You only want to do what's right. That's one of the things I like best about you."

I wish he wouldn't say things like that. It only makes me feel worse. I guess my feelings aren't all that's important right now though. Not when he's practically in pieces.

"Can I ask what happened?" I whisper, holding his hand a little tighter. "As a friend. I'm only asking as a friend."

"What do you want me to say? I owed them money. I didn't have it to them in time. If anything, the wedding was a way to get out of town for a little while and breathe easier. I ducked them for a few days, but it wasn't enough. They were waiting for me when I got back."

"Wow."

"And the whole time, I knew you were waiting for me. I got your message, and I wanted more than anything to—"

"You don't need to explain."

"I have to though. I need to say it, so you understand. I wanted to get back to you, so you wouldn't think I was lying."

"But you were lying."

"Not about wanting to see you though." He turns his head enough to look at me. I wish it wasn't so hard to look back at him. I can hardly do it without wincing. "I didn't lie about that. About anything I felt for you."

"You mean, it didn't matter at all that my grandmother's rich?"

I regret it the second it's out of my mouth. It's a low blow. But darn it, if I don't at least get confirmation from him, I'll always wonder.

"God, no. You don't honestly think that, do you?"

"Honestly? How am I supposed to know? I haven't had a lot of time to process this. But I can't help but remember you bringing her up after the reception. It seemed so out of the blue even though I'd told you about her on the bus. I should've listened to my instincts then. Something didn't seem right."

He moves his hand away from mine and turns his head toward the window. At least I don't have to look at his banged-up features anymore. I almost hate the way I feel about him now. It makes me small and petty.

I don't want to be small and petty, but I am. Like I told him, I haven't had a lot of time to process this.

"I guess I thought more about it than I should have, okay? I admit that much. But I didn't pretend to like you so much because of that. I swear, I didn't. I liked—*I like*—you for who you are. So much."

He snickers, turning toward me again. "Which is why I didn't get back to you. I couldn't risk you being there when they … you know. And now, I see it was the right thing to do. They caught me coming out of my building. I tried to avoid them, but it was pointless. You can't. Not when they're good and determined to find you. If you had been with me …"

"I get it."

"That was one of the hardest things I've ever had to do."

"You could've told me the truth, and I would've understood."

"Right. And run the risk of you cursing me out

and never speaking to me again?"

"What was the alternative? Never talking to me again and making me hate you? And myself? Because I did. I hated myself this whole week for believing you. For letting myself get suckered in by you."

"You weren't a sucker."

"I sort of was though," I whisper. "I believed your story about Zack even though it didn't make any sense for you to tell me something so personal. And I didn't listen to my gut when you threw me off with the *rich grandmother* comment. So, yeah, I let myself get fooled. Though I guess I should thank you in the end. I'll be more careful next time."

"Damn it. I asked who in their right mind would hurt you. Now, I know. I should've always known."

I shrug it off as best I can. "It is what it is."

"No. Don't become a cynical asshole like me. I mean it," he insists after I snicker at the memory of our first encounter.

"I need you to know something." I stand, leaning over him a little so he can't avoid looking at me. He needs to see my face. I need him to believe me.

Because he's not a bad person. He's a very good person. I believe that with all my heart.

So, he deserves the truth if he ever hopes to be happy a day in his life.

"I would've understood if you had told me the truth. I wouldn't have judged you. I might even have respected you more for being honest. And for trying hard to get through your problems. It's not because of your problems that I can't be with you now. It's because I would never be able to trust you again. I wouldn't know whether I could believe anything you said. That would be what eventually drove us apart. Not your past, not the struggles you're going through. The lies."

His eye narrows. "I wanted to make sure you cared about me before I told you."

"But don't you see how much worse that is? You've got to have a little faith in people. I understand; I get it. You don't want to run the risk of scaring somebody off before there's a chance of anything growing. But … waiting until somebody falls for you is no good either. That only causes more pain in the end."

"And it's selfish," he concludes with a sigh.

"I didn't want to say it, but, yeah, now that you've said it …"

He snorts softly at this. "Thanks for putting it to me straight. Really. I needed to hear it."

"I hope you remember it later. Once you're healed up and doing what has to be done to get your life back on track."

He nods slightly, maybe as much as he can without pain. "I don't know what that means exactly. Who I'll have to go to for help."

"You have people in your life who love you, right?" I remember him telling me about his parents, and the summer house in the Hamptons must mean they're pretty well off. I can't imagine how a parent could see him in this condition and not try to help in some way.

"I do." He doesn't go any further into it, and I won't make him.

"Take care of yourself, okay?" I touch his cheek and try not to remember what it was like before. When I didn't know. When I didn't have to see him this way, when he wasn't hurting.

"You too. Try to remember what it was like back there, before this. You said you'd miss that place, remember?"

"Sure."

"I'll miss it too."

My vision's a little blurry as I leave his room and walk straight into a hug from Hayley.

"It's gonna be okay," she whispers, squeezing me tight. "It's gonna be just fine."

I have to wonder. I really do.

Chapter Twenty-One

"I'll say this for your time at that resort. It added color to your complexion." Though, naturally, my grandmother can't give what sounds like a compliment without tempering it with a heavy dose of criticism. "I hope you took care to protect yourself though. Nothing ages like the sun."

"Which is it?" I have to laugh. "Is it good that I got a tan or bad?"

She rolls her eyes. Sometimes, it seems like she's picking up bad mannerisms from me. "Don't make a habit of it. Let us leave it at that."

"Fair enough."

"You enjoyed your time there?" She passes me a plate of sandwiches, which I can't help but notice aren't as tidy-looking as our tea sandwiches usually are.

"I did. What's with the sandwiches?"

"What do you mean?"

"They're usually so cute and neat-looking. There're little bits of crust still on the ends, and there're bits of egg salad hanging out. Is Peter okay?" I look over my shoulder, expecting to see him. Or hoping to. It's nice to get a look at him, to make sure he's healthy and well.

"I don't understand what our sandwiches have to do with Peter."

"Stop playing around. He does the cooking. Even now. And I've never seen the sandwiches looking this way. Is he sick?"

"No, he isn't sick. He's … no longer performing domestic duties. I've brought on additional help since you last paid me a visit."

My jaw pretty much hits the floor. Not that I didn't hope she would do this. I didn't expect it so soon, is all. And I certainly didn't expect her to bring somebody into the household and let them act with anything other than perfect precision.

I've seen the woman nearly throw a fit over something as stupid as a fingerprint on a wineglass.

That was a different time though. Peter has changed her in many ways.

If not changed exactly, he's granted her a sense of perspective she didn't possess before. That's closer to the truth, I think.

"Well?" she asks with a blithe shrug. "It isn't right for him to continue in his former duties. Granted, we've made things a great deal less formal than they used to be, yet that wasn't enough. He will either be my servant or my—"

"Don't say it. Please," I beg. I don't need to hear the word lover come from her lips just now.

She accepts this with another blithe shrug.

"Where are they?" I ask in a whisper.

"You sound curious."

"Oh, I'm insanely curious."

"As any good domestic help does, they remain where they're needed. Which means you would find them in the kitchen if you were gauche enough to snoop around in search of them."

"You know how gauche I can be when given the opportunity."

A smile twitches her lips, though the rest of her face stays still. "Tell me about your trip. I've wished all week to hear about it. Did you rest? Did you have a nice time? What about the wedding?"

I explain the ceremony and how nature threw everything but the kitchen sink at the happy couple.

She's chuckles softly. "I've seen quite a few memorable ceremonies in my day, but that sounds like one for the record books. The bride must have been beside herself."

"She took it in stride. Honestly, it was one of the most beautiful things I've ever seen."

She's a sharp one. Woe to anyone who takes her age as a sign that she's slowing down, even a tiny bit. Her brain is as fast as it ever was.

"Why do you sound so sad when you say it?"

"I do?"

"I do?" She bats her eyelashes.

"Oh, this is a new leaf you're turning over. Mimicking me. Very mature."

"Call it a rediscovery of my youthful charm."

"I go out of town for a little while, and look what I come back to."

Her eyes don't reflect my smile. There's a touch of sadness in them. "Why did you sound that way? What happened?"

"What usually happens. The same thing as always. Only this time, there were bookies and other unsavory characters involved."

I didn't come here today with the intention of telling her about Kellen—at least, not the bad things. It's been a few days since I saw him at the hospital, and I've been doing my best to take a healthy, understanding view of the situation.

In other words, I don't feel like talking about it.

But it's too late for that now. I've already piqued her interest, and if there's one thing I inherited from her—aside from the blue eyes and the icy stare—it's the inability to be turned away once curiosity takes hold. I know there's no hope of leaving the house unless I share at least the basics.

Which I do. Within reason.

There are certain things the woman doesn't need to hear.

By the time I'm finished, she's forgotten her tea and the sloppy sandwiches. She's watching me, studying, anticipating. "And? Have you heard anything else about this young man? What's to become of him?"

"I have no idea. Honestly, I'm not sure I want to know. Or whether I want to keep up with him."

Her stern expression surprises me.

"Is that wrong?" I ask with a frown.

"Not necessarily, my dear. I do not sit in judgment over you, if that's what you're thinking."

"That's exactly what I'm thinking."

"It isn't so. I can't blame you for refusing to keep up with this Kellen's activities. Especially as he lied to you about his friend as a means of determining how you would react when he spoke the truth. I wonder how long he might have left you in the dark if he hadn't been … discovered by the men searching for him."

"Can I tell you something?"

"Always, dear."

It takes a second since I want to make sure the tears threatening to take hold will stay where they are. Inside me, not on my cheeks.

Once I know I'll be able to get through it, I whisper, "I don't know if I did the right thing. Should I have stuck by him? Was it mean, deserting him like that?"

"Deserting him? After a quick dalliance and a few promises of the time you would spend together once you got home? Oh, don't bother." She snorts with a wave of her hand when I try to argue with her. "We are both women of the world, and heaven knows I've expressed my thoughts on sex and relationships with you on more than one occasion. Did you imagine you would shock me?"

"I don't love talking about it with you, in case

you've never noticed."

"You write about it."

"Not the same."

She accepts this with a shrug. "Regardless, you owed him nothing. Friendship perhaps, and as far as I'm concerned, you have not reneged on that friendship. I know you. I know you would answer his call and lend an ear if need be."

With that, she leans in. "My granddaughter is a smart girl. Sharp and wise and clever. She knows better than to become attached to someone with a problem like his. I don't doubt how difficult it is for him. Brutal even. He has no control over it, not now. There is nothing wrong with turning away from someone whose weaknesses would drain you. Not only financially. Emotionally as well. That is not the formula for a happy or successful relationship, dear."

"You sound like you know what you're talking about," I say it with a soft snicker, reaching for another sandwich. Sloppy or not, they're tasty enough.

When I look her way again, I notice she isn't smiling. She isn't even looking at me, her gaze focused across the room.

Where a portrait of my grandfather hangs.

"Grandmother?" I follow her gaze to the portrait.

He's always struck me as being powerful. Strong. Imperious even. She always speaks of him in glowing terms, talks about how much they loved each other. How no other man would ever compare.

Until Peter, no other man has ever lived up to her memory of her late husband.

Now, she doesn't stare at his portrait with love in her eyes.

"I know what I'm talking about," she murmurs. Her mouth is a crimson slash, lips drawn tight together.

"Grandmother, was he …"

She sits up a little straighter. Her hands are folded so tight; it has to be hurting her joints.

"It was not the sort of thing people spoke of in my day. If a man—or woman—had such a weakness or addiction, we didn't speak of it outside our immediate families. And even then, I never spoke to my family of it. My parents would never …"

She turns her face away a little, toward the window. *Is her chin quivering?*

"It was the most helpless I'd ever felt in my life. There was nothing I could do. I was out of control of my life, my marriage. Our money. We could have well lost everything."

After a deep, shaking breath, she adds, "I wouldn't want that for you. Not for anything, dear. You have too much potential. Too much ahead of you."

I can't help but reach out and touch her hand. "I'm sorry you went through that."

She pats my hand, taking another breath, and

then she smiles. "That time is long over. Peter is a good man. Stable."

"And he adores you, which happens to help a little."

She lifts a shoulder. "It doesn't hurt."

Chapter Twenty-Two

He moved over her. Inside her. Driving himself deep. Bringing emotions to the surface every time they came fully together, every time their bodies slapped gently against each other.

Happiness. Hope. Relief.

Love. So much love.

She clutched him—arms, legs, fingers digging deep into his shoulders, dragging up and down his back. Marking him, making him hers and nobody else's. Holding on to him for all she was worth and letting him take her as far as she could go.

"More," she whispered in his ear before nipping the lobe until he growled.

It was sweeter than before since she'd worried they would never have this again. Not only the pleasure pooling in her core, turning her into a gasping, moaning wreck. The connection too. The sense of stripping away everything outside of what was important. The two of them, the only thing that mattered.

His eyes locked on to hers. Lust was there. Heat. Desire.

And love. She would never question that again.

No matter how she wanted to close her eyes, to let

him take her away, she couldn't do it. Didn't want to waste a moment of knowing he was there with her. Really there. That more than their bodies had joined in this most basic and fundamental act.

"I love you," she whispered between strong, deep thrusts that drove both of them closer to the edge and beyond. "I love you."

"Missy ..." He kissed her once, twice, before smiling. "I love you. Always."

Always.

If always meant this for the rest of her life—Trent with her, inside her, loving her—that was more than enough.

Yeah, that will work.

Maggie will surely think so. Granted, she made me considerably spice up their first encounter, but otherwise, she was happy as a clam with the rest of the book.

Though, of course, in typical Maggie fashion, she had to ask for details.

"So? What was he like? Are you still seeing him?"

"He was nice. And, no, I'm not seeing him. He served his purpose."

She didn't like that too much. "I don't want you to think of these relationships that way."

"They aren't relationships. Not all of them."

"Fine. Hook-ups. Does that sound better? I don't want you to think about it that way." She sniffed softly before adding, "I don't think of it that way. If anything, I

envy you."

Well, it took long enough for her to be serious about it. Sure, she'd been joking all this time about how nice it would be, living in my shoes. Being young and unattached and able to date around and have sexy adventures.

She didn't ever come out and talk about it seriously. Not until our conversation after I submitted the first draft.

I'm working on edits now, but overall I'm happy with the finished product.

I guess, in the end, that's the most an author can say. That they're proud of their work. Happy with it. That they did the best they could.

I only wish I felt better about this one. It's sort of bittersweet really since thinking back on the week at the resort makes me smile. The memories themselves are nice, so long as I separate them from what happened afterward.

Is that what I'm supposed to learn from this?

Inevitably I have ended up learning something from each of the men I've dated—something about myself. About my self-worth. What I'm willing to put up with and what I can't.

I've learned how to speak up for myself in a relationship.

How to set boundaries.

How to let go and not attach so much importance to every little thing that happens.

Though I've clearly got a long way to go, since

I'm still smarting over Kellen. He taught me a valuable lesson though.

Don't let window dressings fool you.

"I let him fool me," I concluded to Hayley not long after we heard he was released from the hospital. "The whole external package. The charm, the designer clothing, the expensive watch and perfect haircut. He sold himself well. I bought the whole image."

"Don't be upset. And don't let it trick you into overthinking everything more than you already do. I would hate to see this set you back when I've been working so hard at forcing you to loosen up a little."

"Oh! Is that what you've been working on all this time?"

"Please. I deserve a full-time salary. Benefits. A 401(k), for that matter."

"I'll look into it."

Still, no amount of joking around can lessen the fact that I bought into the image that Kellen was selling. I hope for his sake that, one day, it'll be more than just an image. That he'll grow to be the man he presents to the world.

It comes as a complete surprise when he calls me a few days after I sent him the first draft. I wanted him to see it, to know I didn't paint him as some degenerate. I would never do that. It's not how I see him.

But I wanted him to know for sure since, in the end, we didn't get to know each other all that well.

He might like me, but there's no real reason for him to trust me.

Amazing, how clear things are on this side of things. In Manhattan, in my apartment, away from the beach and the patio and the pool. Now that the giddy flush of lust has waned.

"So?" I'm pacing the living room, chewing my thumbnail, wishing I could fast-forward through this conversation and be done with it. "What did you think of your counterpart?"

"He is nothing like me."

"Oh, stop."

"He isn't. He's a much nicer person than I am."

"He pushed Missy into the pool when they first met."

"She sort of deserved it."

"Okay. Now, I know you're kidding."

He snorts softly. "A little. No, seriously, it's a fantastic book. I've never read a romance before, but your book was better than I imagined."

I don't have it in me to pretend this isn't funny. "What did you think? It's all heaving bosoms?"

"And fiery loins. Yeah." When I laugh out loud, he insists, "That's how it always was in my mom's novels back in the day!"

"Oh, but you've *never* read a romance novel before reading mine?"

He grumbles, "Only the good parts. I mean, I was twelve and curious and horny all the time. A twelve-year-old boy will do just about anything to satisfy those urges."

"I bet."

Darn it, this is so nice. I don't think I've ever met anybody I got along with so well, so quickly. We understand each other. We have a similar sense of humor—for the most part. He's a little darker than I am.

"So, you approve of Trent?"

"Oh, of course. I wouldn't say otherwise." He sighs softly. "Not after what I put you through."

"You didn't put me through all that much. Don't beat yourself up. It wasn't that severe." I almost used the word *serious,* but that could have been taken the wrong way.

Every once in a while, I manage to think twice before my tongue runs away with me.

"And how are you?" I ask since I'm just about bursting with curiosity.

"You mean, am I whole and healed up?"

"Yeah, for starters."

"I'm a lot better. Still a little sore, still have to move carefully. But I'm okay. My parents agreed to help me out this last time on the condition I go to meetings, so I'm doing that now."

"I'm glad."

"And how are you?"

"Well, now that I'm through with the first draft and working on edits, I'm relieved. These new deadlines are getting easier to hit. It was inconceivable to me at first. I was used to deliberating over every line. Now, I have to make quick decisions and move on. I have to trust my writing instincts, I guess you could say."

"That's nice, but it's not what I was talking about. Which I think you know."

It's a good thing he can't see the face I'm making. "I'm okay. I am, really. Life goes on."

"It does. Some of us are lucky it still goes on."

He's not wrong about that.

Does the fact that I'm glad when the conversation ends make me a bad person? Because I'm relieved to be off the phone with Kellen by the time we're finished. I genuinely wished him well—he's not a bad person, not anywhere close to it—but this time wasn't like the others. It's not like saying goodbye to Blake Marlin or Jake Becker.

I'm glad this didn't work out. Grandmother was right. This isn't a matter of him having no concept of work-life balance or being hung up on an ex. Kellen Briggs is in no position to be in a relationship.

Which is a shame because I can't help but think back on his best-man's speech and remember how charming and witty he was.

And how he made me feel when we were together.

He's not the last man on earth though. Not even close.

There's the one across the hall, for instance, who knocks on my door before taking Phoebe out for a walk. I open my door with a flourish and bend down to give Phoebe attention.

"Wanna come out? It's a beautiful day. You can't spend it inside."

"I have to finish up my edits," I sigh while petting Phoebe.

She soaks up my adoration like a sponge, which only makes me want to give her more and more of it. Funny how that works.

"You can finish them up when you come back. You know you have to get fresh air every once in a while."

Yes, and I remember how much better my brain worked when I was outside, sitting on the beach, listening to the water lapping at the shore. I might or might not have found a recording of that very sound to play while I'm working in hopes of recreating that atmosphere.

It hasn't worked quite so well.

"I'll take a walk with you tomorrow. I promise."

"What if I don't want you to take a walk tomorrow?" Matt looks down at Phoebe, who stares up at him in delight. And maybe a little bit of impatience since all she wants to do right now is get outside. Once the leash is on, all bets are off.

"Then, I'll cry myself to sleep. Go on before she pees all over the hallway. Besides, I'm waiting on a call from Hayley. She's supposed to find out if she got a promotion."

"She's a well-trained girl, and you can bring

your cell phone with you," he reminds me as my phone rings.

"Hang on," I say, running to grab it.

"Hayley?"

"Kitty?" It's a squeak. Barely more than the sound a tiny little mouse would make.

"Yeah?"

"You have any plans tonight?"

"You know I don't. I've been waiting to hear from you." I exchange a look with Matt, who's clearly as impatient as I am. And not only because he has a dog who needs to get outside.

When she shrieks, I shriek right along with her because I know she got the news I knew she'd get, but there's nothing like knowing for sure.

"We're going out," she announces, laughing and crying all at once.

"Damn right we are." I exchange a look with Matt, who pumps his fist in the air. "We all are."

Chapter Twenty-Three

"Let me get this straight." Matt leans against the bar, arms folded, looking my way from the corner of his eye. "You didn't have the time to come out for a walk with me and Phoebe, but you had the time to get ready to come out to this place."

"This is different. This is a celebration. You were just as happy as I was when Hayley called with the good news."

We both turn to look for her. She's at the center of a group of friends and colleagues who've all come out to celebrate her promotion.

"I've never seen her this happy," I tell him, smiling at the way she's holding court.

Even with so many people in the bar, she shines like a pure beam of light.

"I don't think I've ever seen you this happy," Matt counters. "Except for that one time when the Chinese place accidentally sent you an extra egg roll."

"That was a good day."

"I'm serious though."

"Me too. You know I love me some egg rolls."

When he doesn't laugh, I clear my throat. "Of course I'm happy. I'm so happy for her. She's worked so hard."

"I don't think I've ever known anybody who gets so genuinely happy for the people they care about."

I have to eye the whiskey he's holding in one hand. "How many of those have you had?"

"This is my first one. But one or ten, what I'm saying wouldn't change. You're so intensely happy when people you care about get a win. I don't know anybody else who's so supportive."

"Remember that the next time I annoy you."

"That probably won't be difficult since you average an annoyance every five minutes or so."

"Whiskey makes you so funny."

There's a commotion over by the high-top where Hayley's seated. I recognize Brandon right away. Kylie and Zack are behind him.

"Oh, I'm so glad," I breathe with a hand over my chest.

"They've gotta be the brother and sister, right?" Matt asks.

"Gee, how could you tell? They could be triplets."

"Seriously. The genes are strong in that family." He lets out a low whistle. "Thank God for genetics, huh?"

"Hey." That earns him a sharp elbow to the ribs.

"What?"

"Are you drooling over my best friend?"

He looks down at his shirt like he's searching for drool. "Shit. Is it that obvious?"

"Oh, shut up."

His laughter is derisive. "If I didn't know better, I'd think you were jealous."

"Of what? Why would I be jealous?"

"I don't know. Why would you elbow me hard enough to practically break my ribs, all because I made an observation? Hayley's got a beautiful family."

"You think she's hot."

"No, I was talking about her brother." It's his turn to elbow me. "Yes, she's objectively hot."

He then looks around, gesturing with the hand holding his whiskey. "So is she. And her, and her, and the bartender. So what?"

So what? I have no clue.

"Just don't go around, getting ideas about Hayley. She's way too important to me to let her get involved with somebody like you."

"You say the nicest things sometimes. Really, I don't know why we don't spend more time together."

I'm in the middle of rolling my eyes at him when Brandon sneaks up behind me.

"Hey you!"

I'm in a reverse bear hug before I know what to do with myself.

"Hey! Long time no see! We have to stop meeting like this."

"I'm just glad to see you've ventured out of your writing cave." He winks, kissing my cheek from behind. "My sister will have to have celebratory drinks more often."

I expect to find Matt laughing when I look at him, prepared to make introductions.

Only he isn't laughing. In fact, his brows are drawn together in a way that makes me think he's more than a little unhappy at the moment.

"Um, Brandon, this is my neighbor Matt. Hayley puts up with him for my sake. And I put up with him because it's easier to be friends with a neighbor than enemies."

"Good to meet you." Matt shakes his hand with an easy smile. I guess I imagined him frowning; the light in here is pretty low. "Your sister will make a great junior associate. Maybe I'll hire her to defend me when I murder this one." He jerks his chin in my direction.

"Wow. You two have a super-healthy friendship. I'm going to get a drink, and besides, Hayley does corporate law." Brandon squeezes me one more time before heading closer to the bar.

"Why do you always have to say things like that?" I ask Matt. "It's weird. Like, if Brandon thinks it's weird, you know you have problems."

"I was only telling the truth." Matt shrugs.

"Whatever. Shut up. Hayley wouldn't defend you if you killed me."

"Eh, you've probably annoyed her enough times that she could relate."

"Hey!" Kylie grabs me in passing. "How've you been?"

"Oh, just fine." I do the whole introduction thing with Matt while hoping and praying she won't mention Kellen in his presence. Why? I don't think I could come up with a concrete reason if I tried for the rest of the night. Somehow, it feels wrong. It would be weird to talk about the whole mess in front of him, is all.

"I'll be right back," he promises with a smile to both of us before disappearing into the crowd.

I can't help but watch as he weaves his way in and out, reminding me of a shark cutting through water.

Though sharks don't usually look as good as he does.

I mean, they never do. They're sharks. I might've already had too much to drink.

"Boy, stupid me." Kylie gives me a wink and a smirk.

"Uh, I would never call you stupid. You're, like, a genius."

She rolls her eyes with a snort. "I didn't mean it that way."

Then, she nods in the direction Matt just disappeared in. "Here I was, thinking you'd be mopey and sad over Briggs, but you're already moving on. Between you and me, as much as I love Briggs, this one's a step up."

Oh.

Oh no.

"Matt?" I blurt out before laughing. "No way! He's just my neighbor from across the hall. I told him Hayley was waiting to hear about the promotion, and he came out to celebrate with us."

"Really?" She cocks her head to the side, lowering her brow in a way that's painfully familiar.

Once again, the genes in the family are strong.

"What are you trying to say?"

"Don't play dumb. I know how smart you are, though I thought you were a little more insightful after our talk before the wedding."

"Nah. We're just friends, believe me. I don't know many things, but I know that much for sure."

"Okay, whatever. You know better than I do." She looks after Matt one more time with a whistle that reminds me of the way he whistled a few minutes ago. "What a shame. Having all that across the hall, and you're only friends."

Now, I'm starting to get uncomfortable, right down to the flush creeping up the back of my neck. It could be the wine though. Wine makes me flushed and warm too. "Uh, that's nice, coming from a newlywed," I tease. Anything to change the subject.

"I'm married. Not blind."

We laugh together—a little tight on my part maybe.

Matt? We'd kill each other the first day. By noon. It's amazing we haven't killed each other before now, honestly.

"How is everything going for you? These first few weeks of married bliss?"

She smiles over at Zack, who's now doing shots with Hayley. The poor girl's going to be in more than a little pain tomorrow morning, but certain things are worth suffering a hell of a hangover for. Still, I make a mental note to grab her a bottle of water.

I'm sort of her wingwoman tonight, though I'm not trying to hook her up with anybody. Making sure she doesn't end up with alcohol poisoning or with her dress over her head is pretty much the extent of my duties.

I can tell from the way Kylie's face glows that she's just as goofily in love with her husband as she was when they kissed in the middle of a tropical storm, soaked to the skin in ruined wedding attire. Granted, I would hope so. It hasn't been that long.

But just like it did that day, the sight of their obvious, open, over-the-top love makes me a little sad. Jealous? Who knows? Just because I don't want to think of myself that way doesn't mean I'm beyond feeling a little envious.

"It's going well," she admits, turning back to me with that goofy grin still playing at the corners of her mouth. "I guess there's nowhere to go but up after a ceremony like that, huh?"

I have to clamp my mouth shut for a second since I might laugh if I'm not careful. I've heard of people changing as completely as she seems to have done, but hypnosis or a head injury is usually the reason for it.

"I guess so," I agree. "I'm so happy for you two. You make a beautiful couple."

"I only wish things could've worked out for you," she confesses. "I mean, so many amazing things came from that week. I'm closer with Hayley. I finally woke up and figured out I don't have too much in common with the girls from college."

"Really?" That's a new one. Hayley didn't tell me about that.

"Yes, it was well past time. I'm not that girl anymore. We aren't enemies, but I wouldn't call them my best friends." She shrugs at my surprise. "Live and learn."

"I guess so."

"And of course, at the end of it all, I wound up with a wedding ring and a binding, legal contract with the man I love. It doesn't get much better than that."

"I can't imagine it being any better."

She squeezes my arm with a little smile. "And I'm happy I got to know you. I hope we see more of each other now. You're always welcome for dinner. The door's open."

I wish I could offer the same, but I've never been the world's greatest cook. "If you like takeout, I'm your girl. You should come up to my neck of the woods sometime."

"Careful. We might take you up on it."

Something on the other side of the room catches her eye, and she looks so interested in whatever it is that I have to see what's up.

And when I do, the funniest thing happens.

I suddenly feel the urge to tear a girl's hair out.

Because she's hanging all over Matt like a cheap suit.

It's none of my business, and I know it. He'd laugh himself sick if I went over there and so much as tried to break in on their conversation.

So, where's this impulse coming from? Why are my teeth grinding together hard enough that I'm afraid they might crack?

"You know what?" Kylie leans in a little, speaking straight into my ear. "You were sweet enough to give me some good advice. I'm glad I have the chance now to repay you for that."

"Repay me?" I'd look at her, but I can't take my eyes off the redhead who must've mistaken Matt for a tree since she's trying to climb him.

"I'm only going to say this once, and then we're going to go over and have fun with my sister since this is her night." Kylie points to Matt. "You need to lock that down, girl. Because when I walked in here and saw the two of you together, I would've sworn on a stack of Bibles that you were a couple. And it made all the sense in the world. You looked natural together."

"He's like a brother to me."

"No. Brandon is a brother to me. Matt is not a brother to you, no matter how much you might want him to be." Then, she nudges me. "If you really do want him to be, which I doubt."

The girl has no idea what she's talking about. Even a genius gets it wrong sometimes, I guess.

"Come on." I link arms with her, deliberately turning my back on Matt and the redhead he might need to have surgically removed by the end of the night if she gets any closer to him. "Let's go celebrate with our favorite lawyer. She's the reason we're here after all."

ABOUT THE AUTHOR

Jillian Dodd is a USA Today bestselling mother-daughter duo made up of Jill and Kenzie—two writers, one pen name, and a shared love for fun, binge-worthy YA romance.

With over fifty books and millions of happy readers, their stories range from small-town love in *That Boy* to glamorous adventures and swoony YA boarding school dramas in *The Keatyn Chronicles, London Prep, Spy Girl,* and beyond.

Jill lives in sunny Florida with her husband, while Kenzie lives in Scotland with her husband and family. When they're not writing across time zones, you'll find them planning their next adventure or dreaming up lovable stories readers can't put down.

Check out our books and swag at www.jilliandodd.net